'What did ~~you say?'~~ **d, his voice gr~~owing~~ ~~at~~ Matty is my~~ ...~~**

She didn't answer, lost for words, and instead she carefully set the jug down on the cabinet, giving herself time to consider her response.

'Like he said, he's been through a lot today and he isn't thinking clearly,' she managed at last.

Nathan shook his head. 'I know what he's been through and I know how it's affected him. He sounded perfectly lucid to me. I want to know the truth and I'll ask again. Is Matty my child?'

When **Joanna Neil** discovered Mills & Boon®, her life-long addiction to reading crystallised into an exciting new career writing Medical Romance™. Her characters are probably the outcome of her varied lifestyle, which includes working as a clerk, typist, nurse and infant teacher. She enjoys dressmaking and cooking at her Leicestershire home. Her family includes a husband, son and daughter, an exuberant yellow Labrador and two slightly crazed cockatiels. She currently works with a team of tutors at her local education centre to provide creative writing workshops for people interested in exploring their own writing ambitions.

Recent titles by the same author:

HER CONSULTANT KNIGHT
CHALLENGING DR CARLISLE
THE DOCTOR'S FAMILY SECRET
A CONSULTANT'S SPECIAL CARE
EMERGENCY AT VALLEY HOSPITAL

THE CONSULTANT'S SECRET SON

BY
JOANNA NEIL

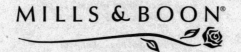

*All the characters in this book have no existence outside the imagination
of the author, and have no relation whatsoever to anyone bearing the
same name or names. They are not even distantly inspired by any
individual known or unknown to the author, and all the incidents are
pure invention.*

*First published in Great Britain 2005
Harlequin Mills & Boon Limited,
Eton House, 18-24 Paradise Road, Richmond, Surrey TW9 1SR*

© Joanna Neil 2005

ISBN 0 263 84295 9

*Set in Times Roman 10½ on 12½ pt.
03-0305-49279*

*Printed and bound in Spain
by Litografia Rosés, S.A., Barcelona*

CHAPTER ONE

'MATTY, you need to slow down,' Allie said, frowning as she watched her two-year-old son dig vigorously into a pile of pebbles for the umpteenth time. 'And don't try to lift so many all at once. They're too heavy for you to manage.'

Matty's chin jutted. 'Me can do it,' he retorted crossly, puffing a bit, and not paying the slightest attention to Allie's worries. Engrossed in his game, he was certainly in no mind to give it up.

Allie watched him, filled with apprehension. It was a difficult balance, knowing when to let go, trying not to interfere too much, but she was always conscious that he wasn't strong, like other children. He was ill, there was no getting away from it, and at the back of her mind there was the constant fear that his tenacious refusal to admit defeat would cause him to collapse through sheer exhaustion.

The tip of his tongue was thrust out as he concentrated on his task, and the plastic spade wobbled as he swung it precariously over the tipper on the back of his tricycle. There was a noisy clatter as the pebbles landed in the bright red container, and in the next moment he had climbed onto the bike and was beginning to pedal along the garden path.

His little face was tense with the effort of getting to the far end of the garden, but he didn't falter.

Reaching his goal, he stopped to empty the load onto a cleared square of earth where the pile of stones was growing after all his exertions.

'See,' he said in triumph, turning towards her, his breath coming in spurts as he surveyed the result of his labours. 'Telled you me could do it.' His blue eyes were bright with the glow of achievement.

Allie smiled, and tried not to show her concern. He was a single-minded little boy, doggedly determined once he had decided to do something, and the thought crossed her mind that he was so much like his father in that.

Nathan's image came flooding back to her in full force, taking her breath away, leaving her shaken by memories, and she closed her eyes tightly as though that would push it away.

It didn't work. Nathan's strong features were still there, as vibrant as ever, his mouth curved in a faint smile, his compelling blue eyes tugging at her heart, but she knew that she had to be strong and put up a barrier. She couldn't allow him access. Nathan wasn't part of her life any more, could never be part of her universe. He had his own priorities, his own path to follow, and thinking about him would only make things harder to bear in the long run.

She looked at Matty. He was digging again, but already his lips had taken on the familiar blue tinge and she was desperate to distract him before he over-did things.

Perhaps the fact that she was a doctor made her fears worse. She knew exactly what might happen to him, and it was so much harder to bear because it was her own child who was suffering.

She saw Matty put down the spade and instinctively squat down on the ground, his knees drawn up to his chest because that seemed to lessen the strain on him. It was a sight that was becoming more familiar to her these days. His breathing was ragged, and Allie recognised the signs with a sinking feeling. He needed these few moments to recover, and it took all she had to leave him be and let him do it for himself.

'You've done well,' she acknowledged, when she felt he'd had time to recover a little. She put on a cheerful tone. 'I think you deserve a drink of juice and some cookies after all that hard work, don't you? All workmen have to take a break some time. Shall we go into the house and see what we can rustle up?'

He hesitated for a moment, but thankfully her ploy worked and the temptation of being able to tuck into his favourite biscuits was more than he could resist in the end. He abandoned the tricycle and went with her to the kitchen, where she sat him down at the table and surreptitiously watched him get his breath back before he tackled the juice she put in front of him.

'Shouldn't you be getting ready to leave?' her mother asked, coming into the kitchen just then. 'Doesn't your course start in a little while?'

Allie nodded, distracted momentarily, her shoulder-length chestnut curls dancing with the movement. 'I'm almost there. I just want to make sure that Matty's all right before I go.'

'You don't need to worry about him. I'll see to it that he comes to no harm.'

'I know you will.' Matty was playing with his toy cars while he chomped away at his biscuits, oblivious to everything going on around him, but Allie was still troubled.

He wasn't quite three years old, but he was pale and small for his age, and the knowledge weighed heavily on her. 'It's hard for me to take it all in sometimes,' she said. 'He's so precious to me, and I worry all the time that I'm not doing the right thing for him.'

Her mother's glance was thoughtful. 'Do you ever think that Nathan should know about his son? Perhaps it would help if you could share some of your worries with him.'

Allie shook her head. 'No. I can't tell him,' she said, with perhaps more vehemence than she had intended. 'I don't want to involve him. It wouldn't work out, and it would only cause more problems in the end. As it is, I blame myself for what's happened to Matty. I don't think I could take on any more complications.'

Her mother reached out to her, touching her arm in a gesture of love and support. 'You shouldn't feel that way. You've nothing to blame yourself for. None of this is your fault.'

'Isn't it?' Allie couldn't rid herself of the thought that Matty's illness was all down to her. No one could explain why he had been born with a heart condition, but she had been ill with some kind of virus while she was pregnant, and she wondered if that had been the cause of his ailment.

Already, he'd had one operation, to put a shunt in place to improve his circulation, but that had only been done as a temporary measure. As he grew it was becoming clear that his condition was deteriorating, and it was only a question of time before he would need another operation to try to repair the defects in his heart.

'No one could do more for Matty than you do. He's a happy, well-balanced child, in spite of his setbacks.' Her mother smiled now, bending towards her grandson and saying confidentially, 'If you're a good boy, and have a rest for a while, I'll take you to the park this afternoon. You'll enjoy that, won't you?'

Matty nodded vigorously. 'We feed ducks? We take bread wiv us?'

'Yes, but only if you rest first. Understood?'

He nodded again, stuffing a cookie into his mouth. 'Me go and rest now. You read me a story?'

'Of course I will, sweetheart. Just as soon as you've finished eating.' Gwyneth turned to Allie. 'He'll be fine with me. You go and get yourself ready. Anyway, you'll be back this evening, won't you? It isn't as though you're going to be away for very long. Did you say it was a search-and-rescue course?'

'That's right,' Allie said absently, still anxiously watching to see that Matty was fully recovered from his efforts in the garden.

'You don't usually get involved in search and rescue, though, do you?'

'No, that's true. Working in A&E, we're most likely to attend to the patients as the paramedics bring them to us, and so we don't get to see what happens from the moment the patient is injured or taken ill. Tom Stanton wants us to get to know how the paramedics operate.'

'He's your locum consultant, isn't he?'

Allie nodded. 'That's right.'

'Why does he want you to do this course?'

'He thinks it will help us to gain a better under-standing of how the various response teams interact. I imagine he thinks it will help us all to do our jobs better in the end. The course is only intended as a brief introduction to the rescue service, so I expect at some point I might have to go out with the ambulance to gain more experience.'

She gave a brief smile. 'I'm glad to be doing it, in a way. I'm a bit rusty after being away from work for so long and any input is helpful.'

'It sounds as though it might be interesting,' her mother conceded. 'It won't be just the people from your hospital who are going on the course, will it?'

Allie shook her head. 'No, there will be people from hospitals all around, but at least it's local for me.'

'Well, you go and join them. Matty and I will be fine, I'm sure. You don't need to worry about any-thing.'

'Thanks, Mum.' Allie gave her mother a hug. 'I'm glad that you're feeling so much better these days, and it's been good to know that I can rely on you helping out. You will give me a call, though, if anything crops up, won't you?' It was difficult being a single mother, but she knew that she was luckier than some. Matty's grandmother loved him and she was there for him.

'I will, but I'm sure we'll manage without any prob-lems.'

Allie turned to say goodbye to Matty, giving him a

kiss and a cuddle. 'You'll be good for Nanna while I'm out, won't you?'

He screwed up his nose. 'Course I will.' There was no doubt, no hesitation, and Allie smiled. He was the light of her life and she hugged him again.

She left the house just a short time later and headed for the hotel in the centre of town where the course was being held.

There was a crowd already assembled in the conference room when she arrived there. The lecture was just about to begin, and the curtains at the tall windows all around had been drawn together so that the video screen, which had been set up on a platform, was highlighted. The rows of chairs were filled with people, but Allie managed to find a seat at the back of the room and slid into it, hoping that she would be inconspicuous there. None of her colleagues would be here today. The event was being repeated at intervals so that people could arrange cover for various shift patterns.

The consultant in charge of the proceedings stood in front of them and introduced himself to his audience. He went on to give an interesting talk, interspersed with slides and video clips, and Allie soon became absorbed in what he was saying. When the time came for a break, and light flooded the room once more, she blinked and stretched, and decided to join the crowd of people exiting the room.

The thought of coffee was tempting, but she wasn't sure where to go to get herself some and she paused for a moment in a quiet annexe off the main reception, trying to get her bearings.

'Allie? Is it really you? I had no idea you would be here.'

The male voice was familiar. It was deep and velvety, wrapping itself around her like a warm blanket, and it took her completely by surprise. She had only been thinking about the man just a short time ago, but how long had it been since she had last heard from him? It must be well over three years.

Slowly, she turned around to face him properly, her eyes widening in shock. 'Nathan?'

He was every bit as she remembered him, long and lean, impressively masculine, his black hair cut in a short, attractive style that framed his angular features, and his eyes were the same startling blue.

She struggled to find her voice. 'I never expected to see you here, either. I thought you were working up north.'

'I was, for a time. It's good to see you again. Let me look at you.' He held her away from him, scanning her swiftly from head to toe, a smile playing around his mouth, and in the next moment he had folded her in his arms and had drawn her close to him.

It was just a brief coming together, and it was over almost as soon as it had begun, but all the same heat rushed through her body as though he had lit a fuse in her. She found that she was trembling, her nervous system running high on a sudden tide of adrenaline, and then the sound of people in the room next door intruded on her senses and she realised that she had to get herself together.

She tried to pull back from him, her fingertips shakily pressuring the expensive cloth of his dark grey suit. Slowly, he released her.

'What are you doing with yourself these days?' he asked.

Allie was still reeling from the experience of being held in his arms. She hadn't expected to feel like this, not after all this time, but it was as though the intervening years had disappeared in a flash. Her body had responded with searing intensity to his nearness, as though they had never been apart, and she was alarmed to discover that he still had the power to ignite her blood and to melt her insides, to make her long for what could never be.

She took a step back from him and ran her palms over her narrow-fitting skirt, smoothing non-existent creases while she made an effort to clear her head. 'I'm working down here, in A&E at the local hospital.' She studied him cautiously. 'What about you? I heard that you had become a consultant. That's what you wanted, wasn't it?' It had been his ambition to carve out a career for himself.

He nodded. 'I worked at a hospital in the borderlands up north to begin with, and then I moved to Gwynedd to take up a consultant post there.'

'Your parents must be proud of you,' she murmured, reflecting that he had achieved what he'd set out to do. He was still only in his early thirties. She hesitated, remembering Ethan and Abigail, and all the old uncertainties welled up in her. 'They always believed in you and wanted you to do well for yourself.'

'I'm sure they're happy for me.' Perhaps he sensed her reticence, because he looked at her in a faintly guarded way and said, 'I know you and your brother have some reservations about my family, but they're good people at heart.'

'I know that.' She said it quietly, not wanting to provoke an argument. His mother might have been persuaded to pass the time of day with her, but his father had never had any time for them. He'd thought her family was dysfunctional, and it was as though they were alien to him.

'It's been such a long time since I last saw you,' Nathan said, avoiding the subject. 'After you left I tried to find you, but you must have moved around from place to place when you first came down here. I phoned you several times, but I could never get through and I thought perhaps you had changed your number. In the end I hoped you might get in touch, but you never did.'

Allie gave a diffident shrug. 'There was a lot on my mind back then, with my mother being so ill and all the worries about my brother. You're right about us moving about. We stayed in rented accommodation until we found a house that was suitable.'

She had thought about contacting Nathan from time to time, but she had known from the start that they were bound to lead separate lives, and then, when she'd discovered that she was pregnant and that there were problems with the baby, her world had started to fall apart. She had realised then that it wasn't going to be possible for her to tell him that she was carrying his child.

Nathan frowned. 'It was terrible, what happened to your mother. I still have trouble accepting that it was so easy for the person who attacked her to get away with it. One minute she was walking away from a cash machine, and the next she was suffering from a bad head injury and fighting for her life. It was hard to come to terms with that.'

'We were all shocked. No one expects that kind of thing to happen, do they? I suppose it's all part of the drug culture that exists these days. It makes people desperate and they do things they wouldn't do normally.'

'How is she now? The last time I saw her she was making a bit of headway, recovering from the stroke. Did things work out for you, moving her to be with you?'

'I think so. She's much better these days, able to get out and about, although she still has a few problems. She was in the stroke unit down here to begin with, so I was able to go on working for a time. I had to complete my final stint as a senior house officer, and I couldn't see any other way around the situation except to have her live with me here, where I could keep an eye on her. Once I found a place where everything was all on one level and she didn't have to worry about coping with stairs, things were much easier all round.'

'It must have been a difficult time for you.' He glanced about him. 'Shall we go and get a cup of coffee and sit and talk for a while?'

'Yes, that's a good idea. I was thinking of doing that before I bumped into you, but I wasn't sure where to go.' Allie was still overwhelmed by meeting him again, and she would be glad of the chance to sit down and calm herself. Seeing him had stirred up all manner of conflicting emotions inside her, and she was weighed down by feelings that could never be adequately resolved.

'It's over here.' Nathan turned her in the direction of a set of double doors, and then rested his palm lightly on the small of her back, evoking a tumult of sensation to whirl and effervesce inside her. They walked through to the coffee-lounge and she was thankful that he couldn't read her thoughts. Somehow he had always had this effect on her, and it was disturbing because she knew that he would never feel quite the same way about her.

'Were you able to manage financially?' he asked, as they settled down at a table in a corner of the room. 'I remember you talked about finding a cottage for your mother where it would be easier for you all to cope, but it must have been hard for you, taking on so much. I know you put the family house up for sale back in Betws-y-Coed.'

She nodded. 'It was a struggle, especially in the beginning, but it could have been worse. I bought a house that was much smaller than the one we had been living in, and that made things more manageable, at least where finances were concerned.'

'How did your brother react to the move? Is he still living with you? I wondered if he would object and make things difficult for you.'

'I think he was traumatised at first by what happened to Mum, and perhaps that made him settle to all the changes. He was only seventeen at the time, and he wasn't really in a position to find a place of his own.' She looked down at her coffee-cup. 'It was a blessing, in a way, because it got him away from the crowd he had been mixing with, and maybe he came to realise the sense in that, too.' She sent a fleeting glance over the table, unseeing, distracted by the fact that Nathan was sitting opposite her.

'So, what happened with your mother?' He pushed the dish of sugar towards her. 'You said she still has some problems?'

'She does, but they're minor compared with what she went through to begin with.'

Allie pulled herself together and stirred crystals of brown sugar into her coffee. 'It was a slow process for her, getting well again, because the head injury was so severe. I think the surgeon who operated on her saved her life. She was left with some paralysis for a time, but in the end, with physiotherapy and constant attention, she managed to pull through. There's still some residual weakness on her left side, but she's made a remarkable recovery over the last few years.'

'I'm glad about that—for her and for you. It must have been a shock for all of you.'

'That's true. I was distraught when it happened. I didn't know what to do, or how I was going to cope with the situation. I expect that's why I burdened you with all my problems.' Her voice faded and her mouth made an odd, shaky little movement. She hoped that he hadn't noticed anything amiss, but he was too perceptive, too intent on watching her reactions.

He frowned. 'Are you remembering what happened between us? Do you still have regrets about that?'

She spread her hands in a movement of futility. 'It

was a mistake. It should never have happened. I think we both knew that at the time. I was upset and not thinking straight, and I turned to you and poured it all out. I shouldn't have done that. After all, you were heading off on a specialist posting. You weren't going to be around to help pick up the pieces, and I should never have weighed you down with it.'

'I'm glad that you did, but I felt bad about having to leave you. I wanted to help in any way I could.'

Oh, he had helped all right. He had talked her through the problem until she had sorted things out in her head, and then he had held her close and sympathised and offered support, and she had been so desperate to share her fears with him, so needy and anxious to have him near, that things had rapidly got out of hand, and a kiss that had started out as a comforting gesture had quickly turned into something more, a fire that had burned out of control.

'You did help,' she said softly. 'After we talked I had a clearer idea of what I needed to do. You shouldn't feel bad about having to leave me…after all, getting involved with you that way wasn't something I had planned on and it was a complication too many. Besides, can you imagine what your father would have said if you and I had shown any signs of getting together?'

His mouth made a crooked shape. 'He's always been rigid in his views. It's unfortunate, in some ways, but that's just the way he is.'

'I don't suppose he's changed at all in the last few years?'

'Not really.'

Anyway, the question of them being together had never arisen. Nathan had gone away and two months later, when she had been established here in South Wales, she had discovered that she was carrying his child. When the doctors had confirmed her worst fears and told her that her baby was going to be born with a heart defect, she had known she would never be able to confide in Nathan.

He had watched his brother's family torn apart by the tragedy of caring for a sick child, and he had always been very clear that it was a situation he could never endure. As a doctor, he worked with sick people every day, and he showed them the utmost compassion and care, but he didn't want to have to cope with the anguish of those situations in his personal life. He had seen what it could do, and he would avoid it at all costs.

Knowing that, she hadn't wanted him to learn about Matty and feel that he was obliged to act as a father to him, and be stifled as a result because he was trapped in a situation that he couldn't avoid. No relationship would have borne that level of strain for any length of time, and she wouldn't risk her child being hurt by a father who held something back from him.

She wondered how long Nathan was going to be around. Sipping her coffee slowly, she said, 'You're a long way from home, aren't you? I can't imagine that this course was what drew you here.'

'It wasn't, although I was interested once I found out about it. The truth is, my brother has moved down here and I wanted to spend some time visiting him.'

'I see.' So he was only here for a short time and

then he would be going back to Gwynedd. Part of her was disappointed by that realisation, but then relief took over. If he was only going to be around for a short time he wouldn't get to find out that she had a child...his child.

Her own love would be enough for her son. She gave it unstintingly, without reservation, and she wasn't about to let him suffer in any way because his father might have trouble coming to terms with the fact that he was ill.

She said lightly, 'What was it that brought your brother down here?'

'A promotion. He's been given the job of area manager.'

'That's good, isn't it? He must be doing well for himself.'

'He is.' He sent her an oblique glance. 'What's happening with your brother these days? Has Owen managed to get back on the straight and narrow? You said he was away from the crowd he was involved with. Has that helped?'

'I'm not sure that he's turned the corner yet,' she admitted. 'It's certainly helped, having him separated from all the old influences, but he found it difficult to settle at first, and lately he's been a bit moody and out of sorts generally. I don't know exactly what's wrong, but he hasn't been able to find a proper job, except for temporary unskilled work.'

'Perhaps that's the problem. He must be twenty years old by now, the sort of age when a young man wants to start making his mark.'

'Maybe.' She was quiet, thinking about Owen's problems, but after a moment or two she glanced at her watch and said, 'I should be getting back to the conference room. The next session will be starting.'

'Is it important that you sit in for the rest of it? We've only just met up again, and I'm only down here for one more day. I thought perhaps we could spend some time together.'

She was sorely tempted to stay with him and throw caution to the wind, but deep down she knew that it would be a mistake to let him back into her life. He was going away, and then she would be the one to suffer all over again, wanting what she could never have. It would be for the best, and less painful, to end it now.

She said quietly, 'I have to see it through, I'm afraid. I'm supposed to report back to my consultant on my next shift. Tom Stanton won't take too kindly to my crying off when he's gone to so much trouble to get me on this course.'

'I'm sorry. Of course, you must do what you have to. Perhaps we could meet up afterwards?'

Allie hesitated. 'I'm not sure that I can manage that. I told Owen that I would go and pick him up later in town.' That was the truth, but she was glad of the excuse.

He was frowning now, and she wondered if he guessed that she was trying to avoid him. He said in a distant tone, 'All right. Yes, you must do that. Perhaps we'll run into each other again some time.'

'I expect we will.' She gave him a wavering smile

and stood up, ready to leave. 'It was good seeing you again.'

'You, too,' he said, his manner remote. 'I'm glad things are going better for you now.'

She turned and left the coffee-lounge, wondering if he would try to follow. Her step quickened and she knew that she was running away, but couldn't help herself. She didn't want to see him again.

Ever since she had first known him, when she'd been just a shy teenager, she had loved him and longed for him to return that love, but it had never happened, and there had to be a limit to how much torment she could bear. There had to be an end to the pain.

So much had gone on in her life in the intervening years, and she'd hoped that her feelings for him would gradually diminish. They hadn't, and now that she had seen him again the hunger for what could never be had returned in full force and was threatening to overwhelm her.

She couldn't put herself through the hopelessness of loving him all over again.

CHAPTER TWO

'I THOUGHT Matty might like to see this,' Owen said, coming into the kitchen late one Sunday afternoon. He was hiding something under his arm, and Allie paused as she was setting the table for the evening meal to look at him curiously.

Whatever it was that he was holding, a blanket covered it, and she had no idea what it might be.

'What is it?' Matty called out from the dining room. He had been playing with his toy garage on the carpeted floor, but now he stopped what he was doing and peered intently through the open double glass doors that separated the two rooms.

Owen glanced at Allie, looking sheepish now. 'Sorry,' he said hurriedly. 'I meant to talk to you about it first. I thought Matty was in his bedroom. I just wanted to cheer him up a bit because I know he's not been very well lately.'

He sucked in a breath and slowed down. 'The thing is, my mate Jamie said I could bring this little fellow over to show him.'

He lowered his voice a notch. 'I didn't think you'd mind, and if you wanted to keep him, I could look after him. I'm home most of the time, so there shouldn't be any problems.' There was a faintly defensive line about his mouth, and his eyes were imploring her, as though he knew he was about to do something she might not like.

Warning bells were going off in Allie's head and her heart sank. What was he up to now? If he was involving Matty it might not be so easy to put things right. She straightened up, determined to stay calm and to try to view the situation objectively.

'You'd better let me see. I warn you, I'm making no promises about anything.'

Owen hesitated, but Matty ran into the kitchen, eager to find out what was going on. 'What is it? What did you get me, Owen?' His face was pale, and his breathing was laboured from the effort of running, but his eyes were wide with expectation.

Allie said firmly, 'It's just something he wants to show you. It's not to keep, so don't get your hopes up.'

Matty, though, was too excited to pay any attention to what she was saying, and instead was tugging fiercely at Owen's arm. 'Let me see, let me see, Owen. What is it? Is it a puppy?'

As if in answer, the bundle under Owen's arm wriggled, and a perky little golden Labrador head nudged the blanket aside, brown eyes taking on a slightly befuddled expression as though he couldn't quite work out what all the fuss was about. When he saw Matty, though, he obviously recognised a potential playmate, because his tail began to thump wildly.

Allie was captivated, but at the same time she groaned inwardly. How could Owen do this to her?

'Is he mine?' Matty's face lit up as though the sun had come out. He had constantly talked about having a puppy of his own, and now Allie floundered, totally unsure of how she was going to handle this new predicament. How could she turn herself into the black witch of the mountains and be the one to tell him that the puppy couldn't stay?

'Oh, isn't he adorable?' her mother said, following Matty in from the L-shaped dining room and compounding the problem. 'Where did you get him from, Owen?'

'He belongs to my mate,' Owen answered, squatting down so that Matty could get a better look. 'His dog had a litter a few weeks ago.'

Gwyneth bent down to stroke the puppy's silky fur. 'He's lovely. I wonder if he'd like a drink of water and a biscuit? I'll go and get a saucer.'

'Can we keep him, Mummy?' Matty's blue eyes were shining with appeal as he looked up at her. 'Say we can keep him... Please, Mummy...please.'

Allie could feel her defences being undermined at every turn. 'I don't know, Matty. Puppies cost a lot of money, and they take a lot of looking after. I'm out at work all day, so I wouldn't be able to clean up after him or exercise him as he would need it.'

'That's all right,' Owen said, putting paid to all her efforts at a stroke. 'I'm here a lot of the time, so I could do that.'

'You're only here in the daytime because you're out of work at the moment,' Allie pointed out. 'I don't know who would take care of him when you manage to find a job.'

'I could do that,' her mother said. 'I'm much stronger these days, and Matty would love to be able to play with him, I'm sure. Besides, the walking will be good exercise for me. He could go with us when I take Matty to and from nursery school.'

Allie hadn't expected this reaction, and she could see that she was quickly being outnumbered and out-manoeuvred. If her mother was throwing in her lot on the side of the puppy, she had virtually no chance of standing her ground.

Even so, there was a niggling doubt at the back of her mind. Would her mother really be able to cope with Matty *and* the puppy while Allie was out at work? She'd only been put to the test recently, in the last two or three months, as Allie had been at home to look after everyone and everything before that.

Owen and Matty must have seen that she was wavering, because they were grinning like two conspirators. Owen put the puppy down on to the floor, and then he and Matty chased after him as he began to dart around the room, sniffing everything within reach.

'I think Owen meant well,' Gwyneth confided in an undertone, watching the pair of them. 'He was thinking of Matty, I'm sure, but he could do with a new outlet himself, you know. He's been feeling low ever since he was in trouble the other week and, to be honest, this is the first time I've seen him looking really happy for a long while.'

'I know.' Allie sighed, recalling the day of her search-and-rescue course and what had happened after she had gone to pick up Owen from the town that evening.

Her head had been filled with thoughts of Nathan, and she had been distracted, still struggling to get over the shock of meeting him again as she'd driven her brother home. It had been all the more upsetting to arrive back at the house and have the police knock on the door just a short while later.

'I can't believe that he would steal a car, as they said,' Allie muttered under her breath. 'I know he was in trouble a lot when he was younger, but I thought he had gone past all that.'

'He said he didn't do it, and I believe him,' her mother said. 'He isn't a bad boy at heart. Everything that happened before was because he was troubled and insecure.'

'I think you're right,' Allie murmured. 'I feel the same way.' Even so, she remembered that a group of youths had scattered in all directions when she had approached, and she couldn't help wondering what new crowd her brother was getting himself mixed up with now.

Owen must have guessed what they were talking about, because he left Matty to play with the puppy and came over to them.

'You're talking about me and that trouble with the police, aren't you?' he said, looking worried. 'I didn't do what they say I did, but how can I prove it? I told the police the truth, but they don't believe me. They got hold of a lad who ran away from the stolen car when he saw they were after him and they think I was the other one who escaped, but it wasn't me. They've got it all wrong.'

He turned to Allie. 'What's going to happen to me, do you think? Will I have to go to court?'

'You might have to,' she answered cautiously, 'but

I'm doing what I can to sort things out. I spoke to the solicitor we met at the police station, and he says he'll look into it for us. I told him that you were adamant that you weren't around when the car was taken, and Jack said he would try to find out if there were any surveillance tapes to show what really happened.'

'Jack?' Owen's eyes rounded. 'You're on first-name terms with him already? That sounds promising. He's young and good-looking, isn't he? Is he your type?' He smiled, a brief little quirk of his mouth that made Allie call to mind how he had been as a mischievous youngster. 'I thought you only had eyes for Nathan?'

'Jack's a very good solicitor,' Allie said, ignoring his remark. Her brother was only around eight years younger than herself, but sometimes she felt the gulf in maturity was much wider than that. 'He's young and energetic and keen to help. You should be glad that he's on our side.'

'I am,' he said, some of the cockiness going out of him. 'Thanks, Allie.' He looked at her searchingly. 'Did you tell Mum that you ran into Nathan when you were on the course?'

'No.' She made a faint grimace. 'With everything that happened that night, we didn't get around to talking about the course very much.'

She wished Owen hadn't brought the subject up, because now her mother's interest was stirred, and it was something Allie would rather have avoided. Owen had only found out because she'd been preoccupied and she'd inadvertently let Nathan's name slip. Owen had asked her why she hadn't stayed on at the hotel until the question-and-answer session had finished and she had mumbled something about slipping away before Nathan could come after her.

'You saw him?' Her mother's head tilted to one side, her grey eyes alert, her fingers smoothing a tendril of soft brown hair behind her ear. 'What happened? Why was he there?'

'I think he was intrigued to see what the course was all about. He's a consultant now, and he wants to get as wide an experience as he can, so he signed up for it while he was in the area. He was actually down here to see his brother. Apparently Adam has moved his family here because his work situation has changed.'

'Really?' Her mother was fired up with the news. 'Well, it's good to know that Nathan's doing well. Not that I expected anything different, you know. I always liked him, and I knew he would get on. Do you remember how he used to come round to our house and chat with me? He used to tell me all about his plans and I could see that he was ambitious, even as a teenager.' She paused, giving Allie a searching look. 'Do you think he'll drop by some time and say hello?'

'No, I don't think so, Mum. He wasn't planning on staying around. As far as I know, he's gone back home now.'

'You should have told him about Matty,' Owen put in. 'Then he might have found a reason to stay.'

'No, it isn't as simple as that.' Allie shook her head. 'Things wouldn't have worked out that way.' She glanced at Matty, who was tussling happily with the puppy, oblivious to everything going on around him. 'Besides, after all the upset with his nephew, the last thing he would want is the constant worry of knowing that he has a child of his own with health problems.'

'You manage to live with it. Why shouldn't he cope with it the same way? You could get together, couldn't you? It's what you've always wanted.'

She winced. Sometimes Owen saw far more than she gave him credit for. 'No, we couldn't get together,' she said firmly. 'He doesn't care for me enough for us to get deeply involved with each other. He likes me, and we get on well together, but he doesn't love me, and I don't want to live without that. As to Matty, if Nathan knew that he had a child it would mean he'd have to take on a burden of responsibility that he isn't ready for, and Matty needs total commitment, somebody who's there for him the whole time. I'm not prepared to settle for anything less.'

'I suppose it's a pipe-dream anyway,' Owen conceded reluctantly. 'His family and ours come from completely different backgrounds, and they're never going to accept us. His parents have pots of money, and we were only like them for a time because Dad had a good job. Everything changed when Dad left us.'

Allie was conscious of her mother's shoulders stiffening a fraction. 'Money isn't everything,' Gwyneth said. 'You should try to remember that. What's important is that we care for each other and we do our best by those around us.'

'Yes, I know that,' Owen said dismissively, 'but we still ended up having to move house, and the Brewsters never had any respect for us.' He was scowling now. 'They must have known what we were going through and yet they turned their backs on us.'

Allie looked at him in surprise. 'We didn't move far away, and it wasn't too great a change for you, surely? You still went to the same school and kept your old friends. Anyway, I would have thought you were too young at the time to take in any of those kind of nuances.'

'I saw plenty. I could see how they felt about Dad letting the side down, and how it put their noses out to see our house and garden start to look run-down. They must have thought we were lowering the tone of the neighbourhood.'

'Well, possibly, but we managed to put that right in the end, didn't we?' Allie was beginning to be a little worried about how distressing this might be for her mother. Gwyneth had gone to pieces when their father had left them, and all this must be stirring up old memories. Allie had done what she could at the time, but she had only been young herself.

He shrugged. 'Maybe we did, but it didn't make any difference to how they treated us. Ethan Brewster never liked me.'

'Can we really blame him for that?' Allie was sceptical. 'After all, he *was* a magistrate, and you did keep coming in front of him because of all your misdemeanours.'

'I was young then, and I didn't know what I was getting into.' Owen was clearly aggrieved by the memories. 'He should have been able to see that.'

'Yes, well, none of this is important now,' Gwyneth said quietly. 'It's all water under the bridge and things have changed since then. You're not the same now, are you? And you've been trying to do the right thing since we came here, haven't you?'

He nodded. 'Yes, I have. Sorry, Mum, I didn't mean to upset you.' He looked shamefaced and shuffled uncomfortably, before glancing at Allie once more. His manner changed, and he seemed to making an effort to put himself on a more even keel. 'You know, if Nathan's brother Adam brought his family down here, it could mean that you'll get to see them from time to time.'

'How's that?'

'Dylan will probably need hospital treatment, won't he? He had plenty of bad episodes with the haemophilia when he was very little, and I should imagine things haven't changed very much. He was always in and out of the emergency room with heavy bleeds that took a long time to stop. I felt sorry for him. They must have been bad, because sometimes they affected his joints and they would swell up so that he couldn't walk very well.'

'I hadn't thought about that,' Allie admitted. She frowned, not sure how she would cope if she came face to face with Nathan's family. 'I hope the poor little chap is coping better these days.' She was thoughtful for a moment. 'It might be that he can be treated with factor VIII concentrate and they could be given supplies to keep at home. That would help to control the episodes and, anyway, as he gets older he might be less prone to accidental injury.'

As to how his family would react if they met up with her again, she would simply have to deal with that situation if it happened. If they discovered that she had a child, there was no reason that they would make any connection with Nathan.

She glanced at Matty, who was still rolling around with the puppy, but showing signs of tiring. 'Owen,' she said, 'you had better settle the puppy down with an old soft toy while I distract Matty. He needs to get his breath back, and he won't do that while the puppy's running around.' She grimaced. 'Have you thought how we're supposed to pay your friend for the pup? He looks as though he's pure bred, and they don't come cheap.'

Owen brightened, seeing that he had broken down her resistance. 'I told Jamie that he could have my CD collection. I've gone off them and he's always wanted to add to his, so it's a done deal.'

'Hmm. Just remember that you're the one who's going to do the cleaning up after the puppy when you're around. You'd better arm yourself with buck-etloads of disinfectant until we can get him house-trained.'

He laughed. 'I will. Don't worry about it.' He turned to Matty. 'Right, little man. You're in charge of keeping watch on our new pup. Go and sit yourself down in the dining room and keep an eye on him while I find him a toy. Shout out if he makes any puddles anywhere. Do you think you can do that?'

'Yes,' Matty said, puffing his chest out with impor-tance as if he'd been given a big challenge. 'Me can do it.'

Allie smiled. She'd most likely come to regret this moment of madness, but everyone else was happy, and the puppy was definitely an endearing little thing. She could see her life was going to get busier from here on.

At work next day, Allie was on the go from the first minute she arrived in A&E. The waiting room was full and her colleagues were all working with acutely injured patients.

'What's happening?' she asked Sarah, the nurse who was going to be working with her.

'There were two separate traffic accidents first thing this morning,' Sarah said. 'The paramedics are still bringing patients in from them, and of course we have the usual run of people in the waiting room.'

'I'd better get to work right away, then.' Allie picked up a chart and scanned the details. She was specialising in paediatric emergencies, and she began by treating a young boy who was suffering from multiple fractures. She worked as fast as she was able, but she doubted they would get to all the casualties in quick time. Their triage nurse was doing what she could to see that the most urgent cases were dealt with first, but it was only when the consultant came and took charge that things speeded up.

Allie only caught a quick glimpse of him. He was new to the department, and she guessed he was there to stand in for her boss while he was away. His back was to her as he distributed charts to staff looking for their next patients, but Allie registered instantly that he had a commanding presence. People were straightening up and taking notice. She didn't see much of him, though. All she managed was a quick impression of a tall man, wearing a dark suit, before she hurried away to deal with a child with a head injury.

'How are you getting on?' a male voice enquired a few minutes later, and she looked up, a sudden edgy awareness making her skin prickle. It was Nathan who pulled the curtain to one side and then stepped into the cubicle where she was working.

She stared at him. 'You're the new man?' she said in a weak voice, her pulse quickening with unease. 'I thought you had gone back up north to work. Aren't you staying in Gwynedd?'

He shook his head. 'Not any more. I'm here to stand in for your boss while he's away on a course, and I'll be taking over from him when he goes to his next posting.'

Allie frowned. Finding him here, in her workplace, had come as a huge jolt, but to learn that he was going to be here for some time was more than she could take in right now. She looked at him guardedly. His tone had been brisk and matter-of-fact, and she guessed from his taut features that he had neither the time nor the inclination to tell her more.

He glanced at her patient. 'How is she?'

'She's responding a little, which is a good sign. I've had a CT scan done, and I don't think we have any major problems at the moment.'

'What about the boy you saw earlier—the one with multiple fractures?'

She couldn't help being impressed by how he had everything at his fingertips. She wouldn't have expected him to know about the boy. 'He's stable. I've admitted him and he's gone to Theatre for surgery.'

'Good.' He looked her over briefly, his expression giving nothing away, and she wondered if her hair was out of place or whether he thought there was something wrong with what she was wearing. She could never get her unruly mass of curls to stay in place, even when she tied it back, and as to her clothes, they were the type of thing she chose to wear for work most of the time, a simple cotton top and a fitted skirt. She could easily throw on a white coat or protective clothing as needed, and she was better able to concentrate on what she was doing if she was comfortable.

His gaze was still fixed on her. 'Was there something else you wanted to say to me?' she asked, lifting a brow in query, and he shook his head.

'No. Nothing important. I'll catch up with you later.'

She was relieved when he had gone. She had believed that she was safe here, with no threat to her peace of mind, but now her heart was hammering away in her chest, leaving her uncomfortable and out of sorts, and she was shattered by the knowledge that he was going to be around from now on. It was the very last thing she needed when she should be giving all her attention to her young patients.

Ruthlessly, she determined to push all thoughts of Nathan to the back of her mind and turned to the injured child once more.

A little later, when the victims of the traffic accidents had all been dealt with, the paramedics brought in a small child, around four years old, who was feverish and having trouble breathing. Allie hurried to attend to her.

'She's not been right since last week,' her mother said distractedly. 'She had a cough and a cold, and then she seemed to get worse. I couldn't get her to eat anything and she was sick all the time.' The woman looked distraught. 'She can't get her breath and I'm so worried about her. I don't know what to do to help her.'

'I can see that she's very poorly,' Allie murmured. She gave the little girl a smile. 'Hello, Jessica. I'm Allie…Dr Russell…and I'm going to do what I can to help you to get better. I'll need to listen to your chest for a minute or two with my stethoscope, so that I can find out what's happening in there. Do you want to have a listen for yourself?'

The little girl was lethargic and not very responsive, but she managed a minuscule nod and took the stethoscope when Allie handed it to her. Her eyes widened a little as she listened through the earpieces and she seemed happier about the whole process after that.

Turning back to the child's mother, Allie said, 'Do you want to give her a cuddle while I listen to her chest and take a look at her ears and throat? I expect it'll be more comforting for her if you're nearby.'

'Yes, I'm sure it will. Thanks.' Mrs Prentice came and stood closer to the trolley bed and quietly soothed her daughter.

Allie examined the child carefully; it was clear to her that she was going to have to admit her for tests and treatment. She said cautiously, 'I need to take blood and urine samples so that we can isolate the cause of the infection, but I think Jessica has bacterial pneumonia.'

The mother's complexion paled. 'That's bad, isn't it?'

'Well, it needs to be treated right away, and she'll have to stay in hospital so that we can keep her under observation. Our nurse will come and talk to you about what's likely to happen, and she'll arrange for you to stay with Jessica, if you'd like to do that.'

'Yes, I would. Thank you.'

Allie smiled. 'Good. Excuse me for a moment, will you? I'll be back in a little while to see how she's doing.' Leaving the cubicle, Allie drew the curtains to give them some privacy, and spoke to the nurse who was attending.

'She'll need oxygen mist, Sarah, and we'd better put her on intravenous fluids because of the risk of aspiration. As soon as her breathing has improved she can have small sips of water.'

'OK, I'll see to that. What about medication?'

'I want to start her on antibiotics right away, and antipyretics to bring her temperature down. In the meantime, we'll send blood and urine samples to the lab. I'll sort the forms out for those now. We should get an X-ray as well.'

Sarah went to organise things and a few minutes later Allie took advantage of a lull to go and take a break. Seeing Nathan out of the blue like that had hit her hard. How was she going to cope with having him close at hand every day? She hadn't expected anything like this and it would be a nightmare to live through.

He was busy attending to his own patients now, and she avoided him as best she could for the rest of the day, needing time to get her thoughts in order. When he finally caught up with her towards the end of her shift, she was putting sutures in a cut above a five-year-old child's eye.

'There you are, sweetheart,' she murmured to the little girl. 'We're all done. The nurse will put a dressing on it for you, and you'll need to keep it clean and dry for a while.' She smiled at her. 'You were very brave, so I'm going to give you a teddy bear sticker.' She pressed the sticker on the girl's dress. 'Well done.'

The child gave an answering smile and went off with her mother. Allie began to clear away the equipment she had been using and looked up to see Nathan standing beside her. He filled her range of vision and she knew that there was no escape this time.

'You made a neat job of those sutures,' he said, watching the little girl move away.

'Thanks.' She hesitated. From his expression, she doubted that he was here simply to chat. 'Do you have another patient you want me to look at?'

'No, it isn't that. I want to know if you can work a few extra hours today. We're short-staffed and I need everyone I can get to stay on.'

'I can do an extra hour,' she said, 'but no more than that. I have to go home and make sure that everything's all right.' She was thinking of Matty, worrying about any time she spent away from him.

'Because of your mother, I suppose?' He frowned.

She wasn't going to tell him about her real worries, and agreeing that her mother's illness had been a dilemma for her was at least an easier and a truthful way out. 'She manages well enough while I'm at work, but I don't like to stay away any longer than I have to.'

His blue eyes assessed her coolly. 'Is it going to be a problem for you, working in A&E? You know we can't always be sure that we'll get away on time.'

The question startled her. 'I realise that. No, it hasn't been an issue up to now.' His manner towards her was distant, and not at all what she had come to expect from him. There was none of the genuine friendship he had shown her when they had met at the hotel, and now she felt a sudden quiver of unease run through her. Had she alienated him completely with her reserved behaviour that day?

Even now, she didn't dare risk attempting to put things right. She had to think of Matty's well-being first and foremost. She said cautiously, 'You told me earlier that you were going to stay on when Tom gets back. Does that mean you'll be working here on a permanent basis, or is this another temporary contract?'

'No, I've finished with those. I'm going to be here for the foreseeable future.'

Her heart gave an odd thump, banging against her rib cage. 'Was it a sudden decision? I had no idea you were planning on coming here.'

'I'd had it in mind for some time.'

'Oh… I didn't realise that.' She was quiet, trying to take it on board. 'I hope things go well for you,' she murmured. She looked at him, and realised that she didn't know him at all like this. He was like a stranger to her, his attitude remote and inaccessible, giving away very little.

'We're all good friends here,' she said, 'and I think you'll find that we all do our best to make things run smoothly. Tom Stanton is a good man to work with. I've only known him for a few months, but he's always been very tolerant and understanding towards his team.'

He nodded. 'I expect he has, but I can't run the department on sentiment alone. From what I've learned so far, the demands on the department are increasing as people move into the area, and they're likely to get worse when the tourist season gets under way.'

He shifted and added in a terse voice, 'I can see that you're all under constant pressure, but I need to know that I can rely on staff to do their bit. From what I've seen, though, there have been a lot of sick-leave absences or people taking time off to deal with family matters, and that can't go on to the extent it has up to now. We don't have enough manpower, and everyone is overstretched. Even with help from the agencies we're going to struggle, but I have to make sure that we do what we can to counteract the difficulties we're under.'

He had obviously taken a close look at the way the department operated, but his words sent Allie into defensive mode.

'I've only worked here for a short time, but I haven't had any time off so far, and I'm sure people don't take time off unnecessarily. Perhaps they're just plain overworked and exhausted.'

'You could be right. What we really need is extra support, but we're not going to get that for some time.'

It was a concession of sorts. She said carefully, 'I can't get over you turning up here. I thought you were settled up north. Has that all come to an end? What about your family?'

'It was on the cards. I've worked in a number of hospitals, learning different ways of working, but I've come to the conclusion that it's time for me to put down roots. When Adam moved down here, my parents decided that they wanted to follow him so that they could stay close to Dylan, and it seems like a good opportunity for me to do the same.'

'I see…I think.' She said thoughtfully, 'You've always been a close family, haven't you? I can't imagine your parents wanting to make the move, though. They must have lived in the same house for most of their married lives.'

'That's true, but they were due to retire, and the thought of living nearer to the coast was appealing.'

'Yes, I can understand that.' She was silent for a moment, absorbing everything he had said. It looked as though his whole family was going to be settling close by…she hadn't bargained on that at all.

He must have been watching her expression, because he said flatly, 'I know that it must have come as a shock to you to find me working here. You were obviously put out to see me at the hotel the other week, and I'm sorry about that, but it was just something that happened. I really had no idea you were going to be there.'

She looked up at him and opened her mouth to say something, but he cut her off, saying, 'Anyway, none of this need affect our working relationship. I'm sure we'll both be able to find a way of making the best of the situation.'

She shook her head. 'No... You don't understand...
It wasn't like that...'

'Don't patronise me, Allie. I'm perfectly well aware
of what happened, and I know that you couldn't wait
to get away from me.'

'You have it all wrong. I was—'

'Please, don't try to explain.' He glanced at his
watch, and added in a brisk tone, 'I need to get on.
I'll talk to you again later, and see if we can sort out
a more efficient duty roster.'

He walked away from her and she darted a glance
after him, her grey eyes troubled. She had made a
mess of everything, and all because she simply hadn't
counted on him coming back into her life.

All the warmth that had once permeated their relationship had gone, as if it had never existed, and she
didn't know how she could begin to repair the damage
she had done. She wasn't used to having him behave
this way towards her, and she was at a loss to know
how to put things right.

It was all her fault. She had destroyed all of the
good feelings there used to be between them, and there
was no going back. She had no idea how she was
going to be able to work with him from now on.

CHAPTER THREE

'YOU'RE being very brave, Luke. I know your ear must be hurting you a lot.' The boy Allie was examining was about seven years old, and he had been very apprehensive of her wanting to look in his ear.

Now, though, she put her auriscope to one side, and said, 'How long has your ear been giving you trouble?'

'A few weeks,' Luke said miserably. 'I had some medicine for it but it didn't work.'

'It all started around the time he had a cold,' his father said. 'When he first had earache, we took him to see our doctor, and he said it was an infection and gave him an antibiotic. The ear didn't seem to get any better, even though we made sure he took all the medication. Then this morning his teacher sent him home from school because he said the pain was suddenly much worse.'

Mr Marshall grimaced. 'Luke finally told us he had caught his ear on something a few weeks ago when he was going through a fence into a field. He thought we'd be cross so he kept quiet about it, but of course we realised that was probably what had caused the infection.'

He gave Allie a faintly worried look. 'We wanted to take him back to see the doctor, but the receptionist said it was too late for us to make an appointment.

Our surgery closes for the afternoon today, and the on-call doctor was out on an emergency that was going to take some time, so we were worried about what we should do. We didn't want to wait, so we thought we'd better bring him here.'

'It certainly looks as though there's a nasty infection inside the ear,' Allie told him, 'and I suspect that the infection has spread to the mastoid bone, so it's just as well you didn't delay in getting help. There's some swelling and tenderness behind the ear as well as inside it. He's also a little feverish.'

She smiled at Luke. 'Don't worry. I'll give you some different medicine and something for the pain.'

She turned to his father and said quietly, 'The antibiotic I'm going to give him should do the trick, but if things don't improve you'll need to take him back to your GP. I'll give you a letter to take to him so that he knows what treatment I've given Luke.' She wrote out a prescription and handed it to him. 'You can get this from our pharmacy.'

'What will happen if this doesn't work?' Luke's father asked. 'Will he be left with any permanent damage to his hearing?'

'He shouldn't have any problems, but if the condition doesn't clear up, he might have to come into hospital to have an operation. I don't think it will come to that, though. Just make sure that he takes the medicine and finishes the course.'

He nodded, looking slightly worried. 'I will. Thanks, Doctor.'

He left with his son a short time later, and Allie

moved over to the desk to find a chart for her next patient.

Nathan was there, and she looked at him guardedly. He was wearing an immaculate grey suit, and he looked every inch the consultant, the man in charge.

Over the last few weeks, she had tried to get back on an even footing with him, but without any success. He had been withdrawn, mentally distancing himself from her, and she was finding the isolation more chilling than she had ever imagined it could be.

She said quietly, 'It must be a week or so since your family moved down here. How are they settling in?'

'They're managing well enough. My parents are still unpacking crates, but Adam and his family have been here for a while.'

'Has Dylan settled in at his new school?'

'I think so.' He reached for a clipboard. 'I heard you weren't happy with the new duty roster,' he said, abruptly changing the subject to work matters. 'What's the problem?'

She swallowed. He wasn't softening to any of her attempts to remedy things between them. 'You've made it too flexible, too fluid on the management side, but less so for the staff. I know you've done that so that things will run more smoothly at the shift change-over, and it works on a weekly basis, but I need my duty hours to be more specifically laid out so that I know where I stand day to day.'

'Can't you arrange for a neighbour or a friend to look in on your mother if that's the problem—or even find nursing care for her for certain periods of the day when you know you might have difficulty getting away from here?'

She shook her head. 'No. I already have arrangements in place. Besides, it isn't only my mother that I'm worried about. There are all sorts of situations that crop up and need to be dealt with.'

'Such as?' He raised a dark brow.

She thought back to that morning when Matty had been tired and irritable. He had been out of sorts and demanding, not at all like his usual self, but she couldn't confide in Nathan about that.

It still bothered her that Matty had been fretful. 'Don't want go school,' he had said, and that had worried her, because mostly he enjoyed going to nursery school. It was a friendly place, with just a few children; the staff were helpful and caring, and she was confident that they understood his problems and would look after him properly.

It had crossed her mind that he might simply have wanted to stay at home and play with the puppy, but his face had been pale and she'd been worried in case his heart condition was worsening.

In the end, she'd decided the best thing would be to leave him at home with her mother, and she'd told her that she would phone and check up on him at intervals. Generally, her mother managed to look after him well enough. She still had some difficulty with her left arm, and her leg was still a little weak, but neither of those problems had been too much of a setback so far in looking after Matty. Their neighbour, Lisa, was usually on hand to give extra help if it was needed.

Nathan was still waiting for an answer. She said, 'There are a number of things. Too many to go into now. Couldn't we just work out a timetable that would work better for me? It wouldn't have to interfere with anyone else's schedule.'

He started to say something, but an emergency siren sounded just then, warning them of a patient coming in, and she was glad that he wasn't able to question her further.

'We'll have to work something out,' he said, walking towards the ambulance bay. 'Will you be free at lunchtime to do that?'

She shook her head. 'I'm sorry, but I can't manage that. I have to go out.' She had made plans to meet up with Jack, Owen's solicitor. It was a fairly fluid arrangement, since she couldn't guarantee that she would get away on time, but she did want to talk over Owen's problems with him, and he had suggested an informal get-together in the circumstances. Over the last few weeks they had become friends, and she was glad of his support.

'Some other time, then,' Nathan said. They were heading towards the ambulance bay when he added, 'I was thinking that perhaps I might go and visit your mother one day. I used to get on well with her, and I'd like to see how she's doing these days. I haven't done anything about it until now because I've been settling into my own house, but things have been going more smoothly for me these last few days and I have more free time.'

The thought of him going to her home, and perhaps running into Matty, filled her with alarm. She said hesitantly, 'I expect we could arrange something some time.'

He looked at her oddly, and she wondered if he sensed her reservations, but the paramedics were opening up the doors at the back of the ambulance and they both turned their attention to dealing with their patient.

At lunchtime, just as she was about to go off on her break and meet Jack, another emergency came in.

'Adam,' she heard Nathan say, on a worried note, and she glanced across the room to see that his brother was walking alongside the paramedic who was wheeling in a patient. 'Why are you here?' Nathan looked shocked. Then he looked down at the patient being brought in, and said, 'Dylan, what's happened to you? Have you had a fall?'

She didn't hear Dylan's reply, but all thoughts of going to meet Jack immediately went out of her head. She hurried towards them. 'I'll work with you,' she told Nathan.

He nodded, already examining the boy. 'Thanks. It looks like another bleed into the knee. Let's send some blood off to the lab to find out what his factor VIII level is.'

'OK, I'll do that.'

He turned back to Dylan while Allie took the sample. 'Did you say you did this on a cross-country run at school? How did you manage that?'

'Someone crashed into me, and I fell onto a log or something. A broken tree branch maybe. It was an accident. My friend didn't mean to do it.' Dylan was looking up at his mother as he said that, and must have read the anguish in her face because he said, 'Don't worry about me, Mum. I'll be all right.'

Allie imagined he must be around ten years old by now, and she couldn't help admiring his strength of character at that young age. The wound to his knee was a bad one, deep and bleeding profusely, and it was clear that he was hurting, and yet his thoughts were all with his mother and he was trying to comfort her.

Megan's dark hair fell softly across her cheek, damp with tears, and she brushed it away, trying to compose her features. She must have been through this so many times.

Sarah was getting ready to clean the cuts. 'We'll elevate the leg first,' Nathan said, 'and support it, and then apply pressure to try to stop the bleeding.'

To Dylan, he added, 'I'm going to go over to the lab to hurry them up and find out how much factor VIII we need to give you to help start the clotting process. I'll give you something for the pain right now, and then Dr Russell here, will take over and stay with you until I get back. Are you OK with that?'

Dylan nodded. Nathan gave him an injection, and then moved away from the bedside, leaving Allie in charge. His brother went with him, questioning him as they walked together.

Allie felt sorry for Dylan. This had happened to him so often before, and he must be feeling frustrated by his condition. He was very pale, and although Sarah chatted to him amiably as she cleaned the wound, Allie noticed that the boy's replies were becoming more muffled and lethargic as time went on. That made her anxious, and she watched him carefully, frowning a little.

Megan stayed by his side the whole time, stroking his hair with a shaking hand.

Allie said quietly, 'I'm just going to examine you again, Dylan. How are you feeling?' He was slumped back against his pillows, and when Allie checked him she realised that he was very cold, and that his heart rate had increased dramatically.

'I think we have more than just his knee to worry about,' she murmured to Sarah. 'I'm wondering if he might have banged his head when he fell. He's bleeding out and I need to clear his airway quickly. We need some suction here.'

Sarah moved quickly to help her.

'What's happening?' Megan asked, suddenly alert to the change in her son's condition.

'I think we have another bleed to contend with, Megan,' Allie told her. 'As soon as I've managed to stabilise him we'll get a CT scan to find out what's happened.'

Nathan returned to the cubicle, frowning as he saw the change in Dylan's condition, and Allie wondered if he would take over from her.

He glanced at her. 'Are you OK with this?'

She nodded warily, but he let her carry on, and she realised that he must have enough belief in her ability as a doctor to feel secure that she was doing the right thing. She was glad of that, though she wished she could be as confident in herself.

'Let's get an airway in place,' she told Sarah. Once

that was done she concentrated on hooking the boy up to an oxygen supply.

'I've had confirmation from the lab,' Nathan said. 'We can give him the plasma concentrate now.' To Sarah he added, 'You can put a dressing on that knee and we'll give him an ice pack to help take down any swelling.'

After a few minutes Allie felt that Dylan's condition was secure enough for him to be taken for his scan.

'That was good work,' Nathan murmured a little later when they viewed the results. 'You did well to pick up on the possibility of a head injury.'

She felt a small burgeoning ember of warmth start up inside her. 'Thanks.'

He glanced at the clock on the wall. 'You've been missing your lunch-break. Weren't you supposed be going out? I can carry on here if you want to go now.'

'I think I'm too late to do that,' she said. 'I was supposed be meeting someone, but I'll ring up and cancel.'

'I'm sorry. Thank you for staying on.'

'That's all right. I wanted to stay and help as soon as I saw that it was Dylan.'

He nodded, and then turned away from her and went to talk to his brother and his wife. Allie heard him say that he would arrange for Dylan to receive care at a haemophiliac centre, and that they would be given supplies of concentrate to keep at home in case of emergency.

She went over to the phone and called Jack, apologising for missing their lunch date. 'Something cropped up,' she said. 'I'm so sorry. I was really hoping that we could meet up.'

'Don't worry about it,' Jack said. 'I know it can be difficult for you to get away. I'm sure we'll get together some time soon.' They chatted for a while, but he rang off when his secretary called him away from the phone to deal with a client.

Allie checked the results of Dylan's CT scan once more, and then went back to the boy's bedside, where Megan was keeping vigil.

'There doesn't seem to be any real damage—no fracture or anything like that,' Allie told her, 'and he seems to be improving since he's had the factor VIII, so I think you can feel a little more reassured about the situation now.'

'That's good news,' Megan said. 'Will he be able to come home with us?'

'I think it's more likely that Nathan will want to admit him for a day or so, just to make sure that everything's all right. You'll find that we have a good system here for dealing with children with haemophilia. Things may not have worked so well where you lived before, or maybe the medical staff weren't sure that you would be able to understand his condition fully and be able to deal with it adequately yourselves. I'm sure that things will be better for you here, especially with Nathan close by.'

'I hope so.' Megan gave her a quick smile. 'I want to thank you for what you did today. You were very observant and quick-thinking, and I'm sure it was because of your intervention that he's safe now.'

'I'm glad that I was able to help.' Out of the corner

of her eye she saw that Nathan was approaching with Adam. 'I'll go and get myself some lunch and leave you with Dylan,' she said. 'I hope that things will turn out well for you.'

'Thanks again.'

Allie went and fetched her bag from the doctors' lounge and decided to buy a pack of sandwiches from the hospital's snack bar. She would sit and eat them outside in the open air. It was a warm spring day, and the thought of staying indoors was stifling.

'I'll be outside in the garden area if I'm needed,' she told Sarah. There was a quiet place out there that she went to whenever she needed time to herself. There were benches to sit on and trees that shed apple blossoms onto the velvet lawns, and Allie felt tranquil there, away from the trauma and rush of her work.

She phoned home to check on Matty and her mother said, 'He's not been too bad in himself, but I think you did the right thing, keeping him off school. He seems to be a little more tired than usual. He played with the pup for a while and then decided to go and get his paintbox out and make some pictures of him.' She laughed. 'I can't say that I recognise Benjy in any of them, but he did have fun doing them.'

'So you think he's all right?'

'I do. He's had his lunch and now he's taking a nap. You shouldn't worry. He's a little bit under the weather, but you know I'll call you if there's anything wrong.'

'I know. I just needed to reassure myself, that's all. Thanks, Mum.'

They talked for a while longer, and then Allie finished off her salad sandwiches, relishing the tranquillity of this small corner of the hospital grounds.

She wasn't on her own for long, though. She was just wiping her fingers on a serviette when Nathan appeared, carrying two polystyrene cups of coffee.

'I thought you might like one of these,' he said.

She looked up at him, shielding her eyes from the sun with her hand. He was tall and lean, and he filled her immediate vision, a dark image against the blue backcloth of the sky. There was a half-smile on his mouth, an intense reminder of the way things used to be between them, and her stomach made a small flip-over in response. She drank in his features with a thirst that was suddenly unquenchable.

If only... But as soon as the wish began to take form she blocked it from her mind, and her heart began to thump heavily in recognition of what could never be.

Pulling herself together, she murmured, 'Thanks. That was thoughtful of you.'

He sat down beside her and handed her the cup. 'You were brilliant with Dylan. I'd checked him over, but there was no sign that he had hurt his head and neck. Things could have gone badly wrong if it hadn't been for your quick action.'

'You'd have picked up on it, too, if you'd been there. His condition started to deteriorate all at once and it didn't take me long to realise why that was.' She sipped her coffee, and then sent him a quick glance. 'I thought you would still be with your brother and his wife.'

'They've gone up to the ward with Dylan. I wanted to give them some time together.'

'I imagine they're getting used to these emergencies by now. They must be constantly on the alert for something like this to happen.'

'I'm sure they are, but it doesn't make it any easier for them. I don't know how they cope.'

Allie's thoughts swung to Matty and the way he would be fine one minute and fighting to get his breath the next. 'Sometimes people have no choice but to get on and deal with the situation.'

'I suppose you're right, but I just hope that never happens to me. I don't know how I would deal with it. I don't think I would handle it very well.'

A wave of despondency washed through her. How could she ever tell him about Matty? She said slowly, 'You see these children at work all the time and you cope well enough. I've seen you in action, and you're good with them. You're cheerful and optimistic, and you give them more than just the care and attention they need. You give them hope and encouragement.'

'But they're not my children. At the end of the day I can be glad that I don't have the continuous worry and heartache of loving them.'

She couldn't argue with that, could she? Her whole body felt leaden with the knowledge that he would never change. With a determined effort she pushed all thoughts of telling him about Matty out of her head. What would be the point? All she would achieve would be to change his life for ever, and eventually have him come to resent her for inflicting such pain on him. She couldn't bear that.

'Allie?' Unexpectedly, Jack's voice cut into her thoughts and she followed the sound of it, glancing across the landscaped precinct in surprise.

'Jack? What are you doing here? I thought you were busy at work.'

'The nurse…Sarah…told me you were out here. I had a client cancel at the last minute and I came over to the hospital on the off chance that you might get a free moment to stop and talk.'

He came to a halt by the bench and gave Nathan a swift glance. 'I'm sorry if I'm interrupting anything,' he said awkwardly. 'I can go away again if I've come at the wrong time.'

He made to turn away and Allie stood up and went to him, resting a hand lightly on his arm. 'No, it's all right,' she said. 'I'm taking a belated lunch-break. I'm glad you managed to get away.'

She half turned and waved a hand towards Nathan. 'This is my boss, Nathan Brewster. He's the consultant in charge.' Then to Nathan she said, 'This is Jack, a solicitor friend. He has an office in town, not far from here.'

The two men nodded towards each other, but their expressions were guarded. Nathan got to his feet, his gaze moving to the way her hand still rested on Jack's sleeve. His jaw was set in a rigid line as he said, 'I'll leave you two to talk.'

Allie watched him go, wondering what was going on in his head. For the first time in several weeks she had been able to sit and talk to him and feel that he was warming to her once more, and now all that seemed to have been dissolved in an instant. His back was straight, his stride purposeful as he walked away from her.

She felt for the bench with her fingers and sat down, her legs oddly weak. Jack seated himself beside her, and said lightly, 'I hope I wasn't intruding on anything.'

'No, you weren't. Don't give it another thought.' She gave him a smile. 'Thanks for coming. I wanted to see you, but an emergency came in just as I was about to leave.'

'I know it's difficult for you. I'm full of admiration for the way you juggle everything—working here in a job that can't be easy, looking after Matty and trying to sort Owen's problems out for him as well. In my eyes, you're a star.'

She laughed at that. 'I'm not, believe me. I sometimes feel as though I fail at everything.'

He reached out to her, his hands cupping her elbows. 'You don't. You mustn't think like that.'

Her gaze meshed with his. 'Well, thanks for your confidence in me. I do worry a lot of the time, though, especially about Owen. I just wish he could stay out of trouble and find some purpose in life.'

He released her, and said in a serious tone, 'I know it's difficult, but you have to keep on giving him your trust. I'm sure that if you show him that you believe in him, he won't let you down. When I talked to him, he seemed to want to do the right thing, but he's confused and a bit unsettled still after the move down here, away from everything he's known.'

'He's had three years to come to terms with the change,' Allie pointed out.

'I know, but he's young, and things haven't gone well for him in the past. I have faith in him to do the right thing. Deep down I think he wants to get back on track, but he just isn't sure how to go about it.'

'I wish I had the answers for him, but I haven't. I'm just as confused as he is most of the time. Have you had any luck with the surveillance tapes?'

He shook his head. 'Not yet. I managed to get hold of them, but they're not very clear. I need to get a friend to look at them to see if he can sharpen up the images. At the moment the youth in the car looks like Owen, but we can't say for certain who it is. In the end, if we can't get satisfactory results, I'll make sure that we have good character references to put forward.'

It wasn't the news she had hoped for, but at least Jack was still trying to do what he could for her brother and she was thankful for that.

'I'm really glad that you're on our side,' she told him, and he sent her a wry grin.

'I'm doing my best for you,' he said. 'I just hope it all turns out right in the end.'

They talked for a while longer, until Allie realised that time was getting on and that she should be getting back to work. She walked with Jack to the car park and waved him off then hurried back to A&E.

Nathan was waiting for her. 'You're late,' he said, his tone sharp, his eyes like shards of flint. 'We've a patient coming in—a suspected hip fracture. We need to get organised.'

'I know. I'm sorry. I thought I was only a minute

or so behind time.' She checked her watch and grimaced.

'Perhaps you should tell your boyfriend that you have a job of work to do. You can't afford to be tardy when patients' lives are at stake.' While he spoke he was checking equipment, making sure that everything was functional.

'He isn't my boyfriend,' she retorted. 'He's a solicitor. He's helping me to sort out a problem with Owen.'

'You had me fooled,' he said tartly. 'I don't know of many solicitors who make house calls, or who sit and hold their clients.'

Her eyes widened. 'It wasn't like that!'

'Wasn't it?' His gaze was sceptical. 'I don't know why you're trying to deny it. I saw him.'

'How did you manage to do that?' she demanded. 'I thought you came straight back here.'

'I did. I turned to go in through the main doors and I just happened to glance in your direction, and there he was, with his arms around you.'

She made a face. 'You're wrong in what you're thinking, but even if he is more than just a friend, I don't see that it's any concern of yours.' Her voice was rising, indignation firing her words. 'I'm a free agent. I can do as I please.'

What right did he have to vet her acquaintances? His track record wasn't so hot. He'd made love to her and then had calmly gone off and left her to deal with the consequences. When had he ever tried to make a commitment to her?

'Of course you can,' he said, his eyes narrowing,

'but I'd prefer that you didn't do it on hospital time. We're rushed off our feet as it is.' He glowered at her. 'What trouble is Owen in again anyway? I thought you'd brought him down here to get him away from everything that got him into bother before.'

She swallowed her temper. 'The police say he stole a car. He doesn't have a licence either, so of course that's added to the list of crimes.'

'What does he say about it?'

'That he didn't do it. He thinks he's being framed by one of the new crowd he's taken up with.'

'He used to say that before. What do you think?'

'I believe him.' Allie sighed. 'I know he's been unhappy with one thing and another since we moved here, but I really felt that he wanted to make an effort to change.'

She pressed her lips together. 'He can't get a job, though, and that's part of the trouble. Prospective employers take one look at his record and they don't take into account the fact that he was a juvenile and that he's trying to mend his ways. I don't know what to do for the best.'

'It isn't up to you to do anything. Owen's old enough to take care of himself.'

'That doesn't stop me from worrying about him.'

The sound of a siren wailing in the distance sent them hurrying towards the ambulance bay.

Nathan hadn't finished. 'What you need to do is concentrate on your own well-being. You have a job to do, and you can't do it properly if you're worrying about Owen at every turn. You have enough on your plate with your mother's frailty, and this can't be helping.'

'I do my job well enough,' she said tersely. 'I know how to keep a balance without you telling me how to go about it.'

'You think you do, but you're under constant pressure, working here. If your private life was to get out of hand, things could start to go wrong. Sooner or later, something will have to give.'

'Then that will be my problem, not yours. You need to back off, Nathan.' Her eyes flashed a warning. 'I'm perfectly capable of managing my own affairs.'

'I hope for your sake that you are,' he said, his mouth making a grim line as he started towards the ambulance.

Allie bit down on her lip. She was tense and on edge, and she couldn't help thinking that perhaps she had overreacted. It was her own fault that she was late getting back to work, and he was right when he said that her private life was interfering with her job at the hospital.

She shouldn't be snapping at someone she was working with, especially Nathan, all the more so because he was her boss. At the least it was unprofessional and showed a lack of self-control, and in the end it would only make her life more difficult.

He was here to stay, and she had no choice but to get used to it. Precisely how she was going to manage things was entirely another matter.

CHAPTER FOUR

ALLIE rubbed at her temple with the heel of her hand as she arrived at the hospital. Her head was throbbing, and it was no wonder after the stress of trying to pull everything together this morning. The last thing she needed was to be late for work again, but that was how things were turning out.

Nathan would have a field day taking her to task about that, wouldn't he? It wasn't as though she could have done anything to avoid it, but that didn't stop her from fretting. She hurried into A&E, breathless from racing against the clock. Her only hope was that she could slip into the department without being seen.

Taking a quick glance around, she was relieved to find that Nathan was not here to see her arrive. Perhaps he was busy in one of the cubicles, working with a patient.

Just a second or two later, before Allie had time to properly get her thoughts together, the paramedics rushed in with a little girl who was suffering from abdominal pain and was by all accounts in a very bad way. Allie went to examine her and did what she could to reassure her anxious parents.

'Phoebe, sweetheart, I just want to feel your tummy for a moment. I'll be gentle, I promise. Have you been sick at all?'

Phoebe looked at her with tear-drenched eyes. Her

golden curls were damp, limply framing her thin face, and more than anything Allie wanted to hug her close and reassure her. Instead, she lightly stroked her hair and soothed the child until she was confident enough to let her check her over. Working as quickly as she was able, Allie took a blood sample for the lab and then tested the child's urine for albumin.

'What's wrong with her, Doctor?' the little girl's mother asked. 'She's been in such a lot of pain, and her tummy's swollen right up. I'm so worried about her. I hate seeing her like this. She's so small and frail, but she's usually so lively, a bundle of fun. It's as though she's a different girl. These last few days she's been tired and poorly, and then today things were so much worse. I knew something was really wrong. Can you help her?'

'I need to wait for the test results to come back from the lab before I can be certain,' Allie said, shepherding her to one side so that Phoebe couldn't hear what they were saying. She didn't want the child to be frightened by things she might not understand. 'Even so, I think that she has a problem with her kidneys, although I'm not sure at the moment what has caused that. Has she had an infection of some sort lately?'

The mother shook her head. 'Nothing that I can think of—except for a sore throat a week or so ago.' She looked at Allie. 'I thought she had got over it and I sent her back to school—she hasn't long started at the juniors, and I didn't want her to have too much time off—but now I come to think of it, she does seem to have gone downhill since then.' She broke off, looking panicky. 'Could that be it? Is it serious?'

'It's possible,' Allie told her. 'Something has triggered her immune system to react, and now that seems to be affecting her kidneys. If they become inflamed, they stop working as they should.' She paused, before adding, 'She's very poorly, and we're going to have to admit her so that we can treat her and keep an eye on her progress.'

'But how will you treat her? What will you do?'

'She'll probably need a course of antibiotics, and possibly corticosteroids to calm the inflammation down. We may also have to see to it that she has a special diet to help steady things.'

'A special diet? What kind of diet?'

'It depends on the results of the tests,' Allie explained, 'but probably one that's low in sodium. We'll be able to sort that out once we know exactly what's wrong with her, and a nurse will advise you on that and on how to go on after she leaves hospital. For the moment we have to deal with the symptoms and try to get things under control.'

'Is that why her tummy's so swollen—because of her kidneys not working properly?'

'That's right.' Allie tried to be patient and answer the woman's questions as best she could. All the time, though, her headache was worsening, and the strain of racing into the department and being flung straight into an emergency situation before she'd had even had time to gather her wits was beginning to take a toll on her nerves.

Phoebe's mother was bound to be anxious, though, and it was only right that her questions were answered as fully as possible. The fact that Allie had several other patients to attend to didn't alter that.

'Because her kidneys aren't able to cope with their workload, fluid is building up inside her. We'll give her something to try to correct that.'

The woman opened her mouth to say more, but Allie said quickly, 'I have to go and sort out her medication, but I'll ask a nurse to come and talk to you and answer any other questions that you might have. She'll keep you up to date on what's happening, and she'll help you with any arrangements that you might want to make.'

Phoebe's mother nodded, looking anxiously towards her daughter, and Allie hurried away to organise the child's treatment.

As soon as she'd finished doing that, she moved on to her next patient and discovered that this time the treatment options weren't quite so clear. She set up an intravenous line and was trying to work out the best course of action when Nathan came and found her.

'Could I have a word?' he asked. His tone was cool, emotionless, and she groaned inwardly. Any hope that he might have missed her late start dissolved like salt in water and left a sour taste in her mouth.

'I'll be with you in a minute,' she said, and he nodded.

'In my office. I'll be waiting for you.'

As soon as she had managed to stabilise her patient she went to find him. Preparing herself mentally, she smoothed down her skirt and straightened her shoulders. She knocked briefly on his office door, and when she heard his voice answer she pushed it open and went in. He was sitting at his desk, sifting through papers in a file and occasionally adding a few written comments.

He glanced up at her. 'I'll be with you in a moment,' he said, signing off a document. 'Take a seat.'

She watched him push the file to one side. 'I know that I was late,' she began, 'but it wasn't anything that I could avoid. There were things that cropped up, and I did my best to get here on time. I was only a few minutes late.'

His gaze meshed with hers. 'I seem to recall that we've had this conversation before,' he said drily.

She stood in front of the desk, and leaned forward a little, her fingertips pressuring the polished wood, her knuckles showing white with the strain. 'We have, but it isn't as though I do it on purpose. I'm doing my best.' She added on a sharp note, 'You need to be a little more flexible in your outlook. Maybe you should try looking at things from my point of view occasionally.'

He leaned back in his chair, his glance slanting over her. 'Aren't you going to sit down?' He waved a hand towards a chair that was positioned at the side of his desk, and she strode over to it and did as he said, seating herself and crossing one long leg over the other. His blue eyes followed the movement, and then travelled up to her face.

A wave of heat rode her cheekbones. Why did he have to make life so difficult for her? It was bad enough that he had come to live around here, but to find that he was actually working alongside her, that he was now her boss and in charge of the whole department, and taking her to task over her timekeeping, that was way too much for her to take in.

'I can explain what happened,' she said tightly.

'I'm listening,' he murmured. His elbows rested lightly on the arms of his chair, and his hands were steepled in front of him. 'What was it this time?'

'My mother's ill. She tried to get up this morning, but she fainted, and I was worried about her. I couldn't just leave her like that, could I?' She glared at him for even imagining that she might do such a thing. There had been arrangements to make for Matty, too, and they played heavily on her mind. He had been fractious and out of sorts, but he had seemed to be more or less all right in himself, and had been keen to go to nursery school to be with his friends.

Nathan frowned. 'What happened to her? What was it that caused her to faint?'

'Some kind of virus, I think. She had a temperature, and she was coughing quite a bit and aching, so I gave her some paracetamol and then waited to see if that helped. I wasn't going anywhere until I knew that she was all right.'

'And is she?'

She gave him a withering look. 'I wouldn't be here if she wasn't. She's obviously unwell, but she insisted that she could manage so I've asked a neighbour to look in on her and let me know if she takes a turn for the worse. Our GP's going to call in this morning.' The same neighbour was going to see to it that Matty got to nursery school, and would collect him from there later on in the day.

'Why isn't Owen looking after her? I thought you said that he was at home these days.'

Allie pulled a face. 'He has to go for a job interview. He has two interviews lined up, in fact, and my mother felt that it was important he went to them.'

She got to her feet abruptly and glowered at him again. 'I should have thought you would understand that these things happen, instead of calling me in here to account for myself. Why can't you simply trust me to do the right thing? Surely you must know that I wouldn't be late without cause?'

He lifted a dark brow. 'Did I say that was the reason I brought you in here?'

Her eyes widened, and for the first time since she had entered the room she was speechless.

He stood up and came around the table to face her. His hands cupped her shoulders, his thumbs gently kneading her flesh. 'It seems to me that you're carrying the weight of the world on your shoulders. You're so full of self-doubt that you didn't give me a chance to tell you why I asked you to come in here. Instead, you launched straight into your own explanation of what you thought I wanted to see you about. I let you carry on because I thought you needed to get it off your chest.' He gazed steadily into her eyes. 'I really think you should slow down and try not to be so jumpy.'

She stared at him. 'You mean… Are you saying that you didn't bring me in here to ask me about why I was late?'

He shook his head. 'I guessed that you had your reasons for that.' His glance moved over her, searching her face. 'I know you well enough to know that you do the best you can in everything that you take on, and I know that you're under pressure. You should know that I'm here for you if you need me, Allie. If there's anything I can do to help, you have only to ask.'

Bewildered, she looked up at him, her lips parted in quivering uncertainty, not knowing what she should do or what to think.

'I'm sorry,' she began, a frown working its way into her brow. 'You're right. I didn't give you a chance to explain. I was so busy this morning, trying to come to terms with what had happened and wondering what to do for the best, and I knew I was going to be late getting in to work. I suppose it all got on top of me.'

He drew her close to him, his head lowering so that his forehead gently touched hers. 'You and I go way back,' he said softly. 'We ought to be able to work this out. Let me help, Allie. Let me take some of the strain off you.' He tilted his head back a little, looking at her searchingly.

She gazed up at him, confusion clouding her eyes. If only it could be as simple as that. If only...

Perhaps he read the doubts in her mind, and maybe that was what urged him to move towards her, narrow the small space that remained between them. Whatever he was thinking, his glance went to her mouth, and then in a breathtaking instant his lips had found hers and he was kissing her—lightly, tentatively to begin with, and then with growing passion, as though he simply couldn't help himself.

She responded with tremulous need, wanting him,

desperate for the kiss to go on and on, clinging to him because her legs were suddenly weak and insubstantial.

She felt the thunder of his heartbeat beneath her fingers and her own heart was keeping time with his, thudding out of control.

The clatter of a trolley outside the door had her breaking away from him. What was she doing, letting him kiss her this way? What if someone was to come in and discover them?

This was wrong. It shouldn't be happening. It was madness. If she let him back into her life there would be no going back, and everything she had worked for would dissolve in an instant. Things could never go back to how they were before, not now that she had Matty to think about.

'I can't do this,' she said raggedly. 'I don't know what I was thinking.'

He must have heard the trolley, too, because he shook his head as though he had been under a spell of some sort and now he was trying to shake it off. 'You're right,' he said, his voice thickened. 'I wasn't thinking straight either. It should never have happened. I'm sorry.'

'I should get back to work.' She was about to back out of the door but then she remembered that he had called her in here and she still didn't know the reason for that.

'What was it that you wanted…earlier, I mean… before…?' She stumbled to a halt, afraid that she was digging herself into even more trouble. 'I'm a bit fuddled,' she managed. 'Everything is going wrong today

and I'm out of sorts. I didn't even have time for breakfast and my head is foggy.' She was babbling again,
and she stopped, looking at him and wincing a little.

'I guessed that. You looked unhappy—vulnerable
the way you were sometimes when you were just a
teenager—and I think that must have triggered something in me. Years ago I wasn't sure how I could help
you, and just now…I lost my head for a moment. It
won't happen again.'

He gave her a half-smile and said briskly, 'You
should take a few minutes. Go and get yourself something to eat and then you'll be back on form soon
enough. We can cover for you for a while.'

He sounded as though he was on form again himself, and she felt a stirring of resentment at that. How
could he recover so easily, when she was still all over
the place? He had felt sorry for her, wanted to soothe
her troubles away, and that was all there was to it. He
didn't feel for her the way she did for him. He had
never loved her and had always been ready to move
on.

'I'll get some coffee and a bun,' she said. 'That will
tide me over.' She wasn't going to let him know how
she really felt, and she would do everything she could
not to show her vulnerability again. They had to work
together, and if she was to have any peace of mind
things had to stay businesslike between them.

He nodded. 'When you're up to it, we'll talk about
signing you up for the emergency rescue team. That
was why I called you in here. It was something Tom
started, and he asked me to see it through while he's

away. There's no rush. It's a bit of a minefield to sort out, because we may not be able to get cover and that will leave us short staffed, but I'll arrange the rota the best way I can to give you time to fit in when it suits you.'

'Thanks.' The news left her feeling deflated. She had everything upside down and out of order, and this whole episode had come about because she had been on edge and ready to seize on any hint of recrimination. She was going to have to calm herself down if she was to do her job properly.

That was easier said than done. Allie made her escape and tried to keep out of Nathan's way for the rest of the day, forcing herself to concentrate on her work. Her patients needed her to stay focused and she was determined to do her best for them.

By late afternoon, she was feeling the strain.

Owen phoned to say that he was at home between interviews and their mother was resting in bed. 'The doctor came this morning and said she has a virus and a chest infection, so she has to take some tablets and stay in bed. He left a prescription, and Lisa from next door went and collected it for her.'

'Thanks, Owen. How did the interview go?'

He hesitated, only for a short time but it was long enough for her to gather that things hadn't gone well. 'No joy there,' he said. 'They wanted someone with more experience, and they didn't want to take on a trainee. There's still a chance with the engineering firm this afternoon, though. I'll talk to you later, when you come home.'

She went back to work, worrying about her mother and concerned for Owen. If someone would just give him the opportunity to do a full-time job, she was sure he would do well.

Sarah called her back to the phone about half an hour later. 'It's your neighbour,' she said. 'She says something's come up and she needs to talk to you urgently.'

Allie felt the blood drain from her face. What could be wrong? She hurried over to the desk, conscious of Nathan's gaze following her the whole time. He was a short distance away from her, studying a set of X-rays, and she knew that he would want to know what was going on.

'What is it, Lisa? Has my mother taken a turn for the worse?'

'It isn't your mother. It's Matty. The nursery phoned and said that he's been taken ill. They seem to be quite worried about him. They say he's feverish and struggling to get his breath. I can go and fetch him for you, because it will be quicker for me to do that, but you may want to come and see him for yourself. Shall I call the doctor for you?'

Allie's heart started thumping all over again. 'Yes, please. I'll come home right away.'

Nathan was still looking her way, and she was apprehensive for a while, until she realised that he couldn't have overheard her conversation from where he was standing.

'Is it your mother?' he asked.

'It's...I have to go home right away,' she said, sidestepping the question. 'The doctor's coming to the house and I need to be there. I'm sorry about this.'

'That's all right. You go. It's not too long until the end of your shift anyway, and we've enough people on duty to cover for you.' He glanced at her searchingly. 'Will you let me know how she's doing?'

'Yes, of course.' Allie was anxious to get away, and she hurried to get her coat and bag. She checked her watch. With any luck she could be home within half an hour.

Had Matty come down with the same virus as her mother? Perhaps it had been coming on the other day when he had been feeling low. He'd seemed to have got over that, but you could never tell with him. His heart condition meant that the slightest infection could tip him over the edge, and it hurt that she wasn't there for him when he needed her.

Guilt washed through her. Had she been wrong to come back to work? She needed to earn a living, though, if she was to keep a roof over their heads and give the family any quality of life. Her mother had never been very strong, especially since the stroke, and though Owen was doing what he could there was no chance of being able to rely on him to help out.

Matty was back home when Allie arrived at the house, and Lisa was watching over him, soothing him as he lay on the settee. His eyes were closed and his breath was rasping.

'I'm so glad you're here to look after him, Lisa,' Allie said breathlessly. 'I don't know what I would do without you. Thanks for everything.'

'You know I'll always help if I can,' Lisa said. She

was a woman in her mid-thirties, sensible and reliable, with a family of her own—a boy and a girl at junior school. Her hair was dark, framing an oval face, and her eyes were hazel and sympathetic.

'The doctor should be here any minute.'

Allie nodded. 'Good.'

'Shall I go and get the oxygen cylinder? I wasn't sure what to do.'

'Yes, thanks. It's in the utility room.' Allie knelt down beside Matty and kissed his cheek. His face was pale and his breathing was laboured, his lips faintly tinged with blue. As soon as Lisa returned with the oxygen Allie held the mask over his face and wafted the life-giving gas into his lungs.

'His colour's improving,' Lisa said after a while.

Allie nodded. 'Matty,' she said softly, 'I'm here. Mummy's here.'

Matty's eyelids fluttered, and he blinked them open and looked at her, not seeming to recognise her at first. Then he said hoarsely, 'Me hurting. You no go 'way, Mummy?'

It was a question, and it wrenched at her insides. 'I won't, sweetheart, I promise. I'm going to stay here with you.'

The doorbell rang, and Lisa showed the doctor into the room.

'Poor little chap,' he said, after he had examined him. 'His chest is clogged up and he's having a bad time of it. Any infection will make things worse for him, given his condition. I'll give you a scrip for some antibiotics, and you'll need to keep him warm and give him plenty of fluids. Let him get as much rest as possible.'

He was a man in his late fifties, and he looked at Allie now and said, 'You know he's going to need an operation before much longer…as soon as he's strong enough, really. It's always been on the cards. I'll see what I can do to set the wheels in motion. In the meantime, I'll prescribe something to help improve his circulation.'

'I know he can't go on like this,' Allie said miserably. 'Thanks for all you've done for him. He's so small and frail-looking… I can't bear to think of him going on this way. He has to get better.'

'You're doing everything you can,' he said, patting her hand. 'Try not to worry.'

That was an impossibility, of course. Allie showed the doctor out, and then checked on Matty to make sure that he was comfortable before she went to look in on her mother.

Gwyneth was sleeping, a faint film of perspiration on her brow, and Allie crept quietly out of the room without disturbing her.

Lisa said she would fetch the medicine for Matty from the pharmacy. 'I have to go out to the shop for some bread, and it's on my way,' she said. 'I'll only be a few minutes.'

'Thanks, Lisa. You've been an angel.'

'You've helped me out enough times in the past,' Lisa said with a smile. 'I'm only returning the favour.'

A couple of hours later, when the medicine had begun to take effect, Matty appeared to be a bit brighter.

'Do you want to go and lie down in your room?' Allie asked him, but he shook his head.

'Me stay here.'

'All right. I'll put a video in the machine for you, and you can watch your favourite programme.' At least this way she could keep an eye on him more easily while she got on with a few things, and if he was comfortable on the settee he would probably fall asleep before too long.

She tucked a soft blanket around him, plumped up his cushions and sat with him until he began to doze. After a while she felt confident that she could leave him and go and check on her mother.

Gwyneth struggled to sit up in bed as Allie came into her room.

'No, don't try to get up,' Allie told her. 'You need to rest.' She looked her over and saw that she was still feverish. 'Can I get you anything?'

'Just a drink, if you wouldn't mind,' her mother said. 'I'm sorry to put you to so much trouble.'

'It's no trouble. You mustn't think like that.' Allie poured juice into a glass and handed it to her mother, along with her medication. 'Take your tablets and just concentrate on getting well again.'

'Thanks, Allie. You're really good to me.' Her mother tried a smile and leaned back wearily against her pillows. 'Is Owen back from his interview? Perhaps he can give you a hand.'

'He isn't home yet. He knew Lisa was looking after you, and I expect while he was in town he decided to look for some things for Benjy. He said he wanted to buy a bed for him now that he's stopped chewing everything in sight.' She put the empty drinking glass back onto the bedside table. 'Do you want to lie down again?'

'Yes, I'm still very tired. I think I'll go back to sleep.'

'Good idea. I'll come and check on you later.'

Allie helped to settle her and then went quietly out of the room. Matty had fallen asleep and she decided to go into the kitchen to start on a few chores.

The doorbell rang as she finished wiping down the work surfaces, and she guessed it must be Owen at last. He was always forgetting his key.

Pulling open the front door, she said, 'Did you get held up in town? I thought you—' And then with a sense of shock she realised that it wasn't Owen standing there but Nathan.

Open-mouthed, she stared at him. 'Nathan? I didn't realise it was you. I was expecting Owen.'

His mouth twisted. 'So I gathered. May I come in? I hoped I might find out how Gwyneth is doing. I was concerned for her when you rushed away this afternoon.'

'My mother? Oh, yes…she's much better now. The antibiotics seem to be working at last and she's sleeping.'

'I'm glad about that. That's probably the best medicine after all.' He waited, raising a brow. 'Aren't you going to invite me in? We could stand here and talk, I suppose, but I wouldn't say no to a cup of coffee. I was held up at the hospital, and I've only just managed to get away. I promise I won't disturb Gwyneth if she's resting.'

'I… Yes, of course.' Allie didn't see how she could shut the door on him, but all the same she was all too aware that Matty was in the living room and she was desperately searching for a get-out. 'How did you find out where I live?' she asked.

'Sarah told me. She gave me a letter and asked me if I would pass it on to you. Apparently your friend Jack left it with her at lunchtime, when you were out, and she forgot to give it to you.'

'Oh, I see.' Jack had promised her a summary of what he had managed to come up with for Owen's forthcoming court appearance, but it didn't look as though Nathan was going to hand it to her on the doorstep, and she couldn't see any way round the situation except to let him in.

'I'll take you through to the kitchen,' she said, 'and I'll put the kettle on.' Perhaps she could keep him in there and avoid showing him around. With any luck Matty would stay asleep on the settee and Nathan need never know that he was there.

Nathan put Jack's letter down on the kitchen table and looked around. 'This is lovely,' he said, his glance straying over the cream-coloured kitchen units and the wood-block worktops that were her pride and joy. 'It's warm and bright, and the tiles are perfect, just the right blend of colours. Was it like this when you moved in, or did you add to it?'

'I added the worktops,' Allie said, 'and the tiles. Everything else in the kitchen is as it was when we bought the house. It isn't up to your standard, of course, but I doubt we'll ever be able to match what you're used to.'

He frowned. 'Why do you say that? My parents' home is grand, I admit—they've always had the best of everything—but I've just bought a place of my own down here, and I'd be happy if it was half as homely as what I've seen here so far. Even your hallway is welcoming.' He glanced at her, his mouth making a wry twist. 'More so than you are, but perhaps I've caught you at a bad time.'

Allie gave a brief, awkward smile in response. She was still eaten up with tension, afraid of what he might discover, but he was looking out of the window now and didn't appear fazed by her lack of warmth.

He said softly, 'Your garden looks good, too, but, then, you always did crave masses of flowers and plenty of lawn.'

She almost blurted out that Matty loved the space out there, but stopped herself in time. His brows drew together a moment later, though, and when she followed the direction of his gaze, she realised that he had caught sight of Benjy exploring the rockery. The puppy's tail was wagging with joyful enthusiasm, and she guessed he must have caught sight of a toy Matty had dropped there.

'I didn't realise you had a puppy,' Nathan said. 'He can't be very old…a few weeks maybe? Is he yours?'

'He belongs to Owen. You know how he is with animals. He can't resist them, and they seem to get on well with him, too.'

'That's true. He's always had a soft spot for them, hasn't he? I remember some years ago he showed me a baby bird he'd nursed back to health. He kept it in a box and fed it fluids through an eye-dropper, didn't he?'

She nodded. Laughing, she said, 'He wanted me to help him collect worms for it, but I drew the line at that. When it was stronger he put it back near the nest it had fallen from and watched it learn to fly.'

She stared wistfully out at the garden, but the view no longer registered with her. 'He hasn't changed as far as that goes. He's always longed to have a pet of his own.'

Frowning, she said, 'Looking back, I suppose it must have started after Dad left us. Owen was only seven when that happened and his world collapsed around him overnight. Mum went to pieces, and had a nervous breakdown… I didn't see it at the time, but I imagine Owen was desperate for something to hold onto, something to cherish.'

'You were always there for him.'

She shook her head. 'I don't think I handled things too well. I was only a teenager myself, and I was as confused as he was.'

'But you stayed, and you looked out for him when your mother wasn't able to. You made sure that there was food on the table and that he had clean clothes to wear. I remember when he hurt himself you were the first one he turned to. You were the one steadfast element in his life.'

'Maybe.' The kettle boiled and she went to make coffee. 'Are you hungry? Did you manage to get a meal at the hospital?'

He shook his head. 'There wasn't time. We had to

deal with a road traffic accident after you left, and we were all working flat out.'

'I'm sorry.' The suddenness of her leaving must have left the department in a vulnerable position.

She reached into a cupboard for plates and set out a snack from leftovers in the fridge—salad and cheese, some bread rolls and butter. 'Help yourself,' she said.

She had been so busy looking after her mother and Matty since she'd arrived home that she had forgotten to get herself something to eat, and now her stomach was complaining. Or perhaps it was just nerves, seeing Nathan in her kitchen.

He started to eat with relish, and she turned away to wipe her hands on a towel. When she looked back at him just a short time later, though, it felt as though her heart had stopped.

He was staring at the small figure that had appeared in the kitchen doorway. Still drowsy from sleep, Matty was standing there, trailing his comfort blanket alongside him.

'Me thirsty,' Matty said, rubbing his eyes. 'Me want drink.' Then he looked curiously up at Nathan. 'Who dat man, Mummy?'

CHAPTER FIVE

ALLIE'S mouth went dry with shock. This was what she had feared, and now she could see no way round the situation. Matty was standing in the doorway and Nathan was looking as though he'd been knocked for six.

She bent to swoop Matty up in her arms. 'I'll get you a drink of milk,' she said, 'and some cookies. You know, Matty, you shouldn't be wandering about like this. You've been poorly and you need to go and sit down and rest.' She kissed him on the cheek and realised that he was slightly feverish. 'Tell you what—I'll take you through to the dining room and you can sit in the rocking chair if you want.'

It had always been his favourite chair, and Matty nodded eagerly.

Conscious of Nathan following her every move, she took Matty through to the next room and settled him down, handing him a picture book and a cuddly teddy that he had left on the table earlier that day.

'Stay there and look at your book while I fetch you a drink and your medicine.' At least with the glass doors pulled open she could keep an eye on him through the archway from the kitchen while she did that.

'Who dat man?' Matty said again, yawning, and she swallowed, not sure what she should tell him.

'He's a friend, from work.'

He seemed to be happy enough with that, and began to slowly turn the pages of his book. She noticed that he was trying to keep his eyes open against all the odds so that he could take in the colourful pictures. He was still sleepy, and she guessed the medication he had taken a few hours ago was having an effect on him, though it was getting late now and was very near his bedtime. At least his breathing had improved.

Going back into the kitchen, she cast a wary glance at Nathan. He still looked shocked, his face pale and tense, as though he wasn't quite able to take it in.

'He's your son?' he asked.

She nodded, going over to the fridge and taking out a bottle of milk. She didn't trust herself to speak. Her nerves were jumping all over the place, and it took all she had to stop her hands from shaking.

'When you and I made love...I assumed there were no repercussions... You would have told me if there had been, wouldn't you?'

He was watching her closely, on full alert, and she had to steel herself not to give anything away. She had come too far to change things now. It had been madness to think that she could keep him from learning that she had a child, but he didn't have to know that Matty was his.

'I would have told you if there was anything you needed to know.'

'So he isn't mine?'

'Relax,' she said, and she marvelled at the way she managed to keep her voice calm. 'You don't have to worry about that.'

She could see that he wasn't convinced. He said carefully, 'How old is he?'

'He's two.' Matty was nearer to three, but he was small for his years and perhaps Nathan wouldn't be able to work out his true age. She knew that he was trying to make sense of things, and from his expression she guessed he was making some mental calculations to check what she was saying.

Matty had the same dark hair as Nathan, and blue eyes, but his features weren't as sharply sculpted. Maybe when he was older there would be a similarity between them, but it wasn't too obvious just yet, and right now she was thankful for that.

'I hadn't realised that you were involved with someone.' His jaw was taut, his mouth a straight line. 'Where's the child's father? Does he live here with you?'

She gave a light, awkward shrug. 'He hasn't stayed around.'

He glanced at her hand and saw that it was ringless. 'You didn't want to marry him?'

'Things didn't work out that way.'

His eyes narrowed on her. 'Why didn't you tell me that you had a son?'

It was yet another question that she had hoped she wouldn't have to answer. 'I didn't want to make matters worse.' She pulled in a quick breath and added hastily, 'When I wanted to go back to work a few months ago, there was a lot of competition around. At my interview they didn't ask me about family, and I thought it would be wiser to keep quiet about it. I know it shouldn't make a difference to employers but

I didn't want to take any chances. I was worried that I might lose the opportunity of a job because people would assume that my family commitments might get in the way.'

'But you didn't tell me. Aren't I more to you than just a boss?'

'Yes, of course…but I…' She had to think quickly. 'You were quizzing me about why I couldn't work overtime, and tackling me about the duty roster and why I couldn't be more flexible in my work schedule… I need this job, and I thought it would make things more difficult if you knew.'

His expression was grim. 'You must think I'm heartless. Surely there are more important things in life than duty rosters. As far as I was concerned, you were young, free and single, with nothing to stop you from being flexible.'

He didn't say any more but stared bleakly towards the dining room, and she guessed that he was still trying to take it all in. He watched her take a bottle of antibiotic medicine from a cupboard and frowned.

'Is he ill?'

'He has a chest infection,' she murmured, adding awkwardly, 'I'll take his drink through to him and settle him down.'

He nodded. She went into the dining room and gave Matty a spoon of his medicine and helped him with his cup. Then, when he had drunk all he wanted, she settled him back in his seat. His eyelids were drooping once more, and she said softly, 'I'm going to take you to bed in a little while, sweetheart. I think you'll feel much better in the morning when you've had a good night's sleep. Five more minutes.'

He nodded drowsily, and she went back to the kitchen.

Nathan was standing by the window, but he turned as she entered the room and said, 'Was it a fabrication when you told me that Gwyneth was ill?'

She shook her head. 'No. They're both ill. My mother has never been very strong, and, as to Matty, young children pick up infections fairly easily.'

He nodded, as though he was satisfied by that answer, and then asked softly, 'Did you call him Matty after his grandfather...your mother's father? His name was Matthew, wasn't it?'

'That's right. I was very fond of him, and of my grandmother.' She glanced at him, wariness clouding her eyes. 'I really should get Matty into bed, and I need to check on my mother again.'

His mouth made a straight line. 'I'll go,' he said, 'and leave you to it. I can see that I'm in the way here.'

That sounded so stark, as though he felt that she was trying to get rid of him, and guilt for her deception was eating away at her.

'It isn't that... It's just that things are difficult for me. It's hard for me to know what to do for the best. Some days I feel as though I have to split myself so many ways, and there's Owen to think of, too. He'll be home soon, and I suspect he'll have had a difficult day as well.'

She guessed that Owen hadn't been successful at either of his interviews, or he would have come rushing home to tell her his news. Each rejection chipped away at his self-confidence and she felt the pain along with him.

'That's another problem you could do without,' Nathan said, his mouth making a grim shape. 'He ought to have learned to stay out of trouble by now.'

'I don't believe he's done anything wrong. You think badly of him because of the way he used to be. He's changed. I know he has.'

He wasn't convinced. 'They say mud sticks, don't they? I'd be more inclined to believe in him if the police weren't involved all over again.'

Her chin lifted. 'He's my brother and I love him, and I'll stand by him come what may.'

'Haven't you always?' Nathan started towards the door. 'I've no idea what your plans are, but you had better take some time off to take care of your family. There's no point in struggling in to work when your mind will be back here. No matter what arrangements you make, you'll be worrying about what's going on and your mind won't be on your job. In our work you need to be on top of everything.'

'You'll be short-handed, won't you?'

He nodded. 'We'll manage somehow.'

She saw him out, a sense of defeat and anxiety pervading her nervous system. How long could she manage to keep up this wall of defence? How long would it be before she was forced to tell him the truth about her situation? Already he was shocked to learn that she had a child, and even now he was counting the cost of that against her ability to do her job properly. Wouldn't he be completely horrified if he was to discover that Matty was his son, and that he was desperately ill?

Owen came home just a few minutes later, and Allie could see that things had gone badly for him. His shoulders were slumped, and even though he showed her the bed he had bought for Benjy, and a jigsaw puzzle that was just right for Matty, he looked down in the mouth.

'You've done well there,' she murmured. 'Matty will love the puzzle and the bed is just the right size for Benjy.'

'I was lucky. I went into a couple of charity shops and I managed to pick them up for next to nothing.'

'That's good.'

'Yes, but I wish I could help out more financially. I don't see how I'm going to be able to do that any time soon, though. No one seems to want to employ me.'

'Don't be so hard on yourself. Something will turn up. You have to keep trying, that's all.'

He grimaced. 'That's all very well, providing nothing comes of the court case.' He sighed. 'How's Mum? Is she any better? Lisa said she would keep an eye on her until you came home if I wanted to go into town.'

'She's not doing too badly. She was a bit hot when I went in to see her last, but it will take time for the medication to work.'

'I suppose Matty's in bed by now?'

'Yes. He's gone down with an infection as well, so we have to be extra careful with him over the next week or so.'

Owen looked concerned. 'Is it another chest infection?' Allie nodded, and he winced. 'They always affect him badly, don't they? Do you want me to stay home and look after him tomorrow?'

'No, I'd better do that. He thinks the world of you, but he's been fretful today and he'll probably be happier if I'm with him when he's poorly. Besides, I want to make sure that nothing untoward happens. Thanks for offering, though.'

'That's all right. If you're not going to need me around here I'll probably go back into town instead in the afternoon and see if any more job vacancies have come in.'

'That sounds like a good idea. Try not to let things get you down.'

It was easier to give the advice than to follow it herself. Next day, when she'd hoped things would be looking up all round, she realised that her mother was having a relapse and Matty was more fretful than ever. Owen had gone out, as he had said he would, and Allie had her hands full trying to cope with two invalids. In the end she called her GP and asked him to visit.

'I was planning on coming to see Matty again anyway,' he told her as he went into the living room where Matty was lying on the settee. 'I was worried about the little man. I'll look at him first, shall I? And then go and see your mother?'

'Thanks. I think the antibiotic's beginning to get to grips with Matty's infection, but being ill is adding to the strain on his heart.'

The doctor went to examine him, talking to him cheerfully the whole time, and then he stood up and took Allie to one side. 'I'm sure you're right. He's finding it difficult at the moment, but all you can do is keep him quiet and let him rest, and give him oxygen when you feel that he needs it. I'll adjust the dosage of his medication to try to improve his circulation a little more.'

'Did you look into the possibility of him having surgery?'

He nodded. 'I did. I made a few phone calls and he's been moved up the list, but there's still going to be a bit of a wait because Cardiology doesn't have as many paediatric surgeons as are needed, and the operating schedules are stretched for various reasons. I'll do what I can to move Matty even further up the list, but he needs to be stronger before he can undergo surgery anyway.'

He moved towards the door. 'Now, about your mother. You say she isn't improving?'

'She's taken a turn for the worse, and I've been wondering if she needs a different antibiotic, perhaps one with a broader spectrum?'

He nodded. 'It's a possibility. I know your judgement isn't usually far out, Allie. I'll go and have a look at her.'

He came back a few minutes later. 'I've written out another prescription for her, and I've given her a couple of tablets now, to keep her going until you can get the prescription filled. I know it's going to be difficult for you to get away right now.'

'Thanks, Ben.' She saw him out to his car, thankful that she had a GP she could rely on. He was more than just a doctor; she had come to think of him as a friend.

By evening, Allie was feeling thoroughly frazzled. Owen hadn't come home yet, and she was run ragged between worrying about the invalids and looking after the puppy, who seemed totally unable to keep out of mischief. He had taken to pulling items out of her wash basket, and as she rescued yet another of Matty's socks and threw the chewed remnants into the bin, she sighed and ran a hand through her hair.

The doorbell sounded, and she guessed it was her brother and went to let him in. She was startled to see that his friend, Sam, was with him—supporting him, in fact, since he seemed incapable of walking by himself. She stared in disbelief and horror as the friend took him through to the dining room and eased him down into a chair.

'Sorry about that,' the youth said, looking sheepish. 'He came back to my place and we had a bit to drink. A bit too much, really. He doesn't look too good, though, so I thought I'd better bring him home.'

Allie knelt down beside Owen. He was breathing fitfully, and he looked ill. He wasn't answering any of her questions, or showing any sign of recognition, and when she checked his pulse she discovered that it was far too fast. She was alarmed, seeing him this way. She stood up, running her hands down her jeans, giving herself a moment to think.

'I'm glad you brought him here,' she told Sam. 'How much has he had to drink?'

He shrugged. 'Don't know. We was kind of drowning our sorrows. He didn't have any luck with the jobs and I had my motorbike nicked.'

Allie looked at him. 'Where did you get the money for the drink?'

'We didn't. My dad's gone away for the weekend and he left the cupboard unlocked, so I helped myself.'

'Won't he mind?'

'Nah…shouldn't think so. He's a bit of a drinker himself.' He sent her an awkward look. 'I'd better be going. I should clean up a bit. Owen was sick and his eyes went a bit odd. I thought he was going to start having a fit on me. I'll leave you to sort him out, shall I? I expect you'll know what to do, being a doctor and all.'

Allie pulled in a deep breath and went with Sam to the door. Could this day get any worse? She watched him saunter away. About to shut the front door, she saw that Nathan had pulled up in his car, and the next moment he had climbed out of the silver saloon and was coming towards her.

'You look as though you've seen a ghost,' he said. 'Are you OK? Who was that—one of Owen's friends? Has he upset you?'

'I'm not sure if I'm OK or not,' she answered thinly. 'He's just brought Owen home, and from the looks of him Owen's in a bad way. He's been drinking and he isn't used to it. I need to go and check on him. You'd better come in.'

They went into the dining room and Nathan took everything in at a glance. 'I'll deal with this,' he said. 'He doesn't look too good, and you're about at the end of your tether. Will you get my medical bag from the car?' He tossed her the keys. 'I've a ventilation kit in there, among other things.'

She hurried away to fetch what he needed, and when she came back he said, 'We need to rehydrate him. I'll check his blood glucose, but I'm pretty sure he'll need glucose IV.'

He worked swiftly, while Allie acted as his assistant. She was finding it hard to take everything in. She followed his instructions blindly, hurrying to get whatever he needed, and all the time she felt as though she was removed from the situation. She ought to have known what to do, but it was as though she was numb inside and every part of her was chilled and unable to act properly.

After a time, she roused herself to ask, 'Should we get him to hospital?'

He shook his head. 'I don't think it will come to that. He's been convulsing, but things are beginning to settle down. It'll take him a while to come round, but I think he's going to be all right. I'm sure he's out of danger now.'

She nodded, relieved. 'I'll go and check on Matty and my mother and then I'll put the kettle on.'

'Are they no better? I was hoping that you might have some good news for me today.'

She shook her head. 'It's been a bad day all round.'

She came back into the dining room after a while and said, 'I've made a pot of tea. Do you think he'll be OK if you leave him for a minute or two? I can stay with him while you get a drink.' She bit her lip. 'I'm sorry you had to come here and deal with this. It wasn't your problem. I should have been the one to see to him.'

'You did what you could.' Nathan stood up and came over to her. 'He'll be fine while we both take a break. Are the others all right?'

'Yes, I think so, for now.'

She followed him into the kitchen as though she was shell-shocked and watched as he went over to the sink and washed his hands.

'I shouldn't have left you to it,' she said, passing him a towel when he was done. 'I don't know what's wrong with me. I feel as though I'm in the middle of a nightmare, but I deal with situations that are much worse than this when I'm at work.'

He dried his hands and put the towel to one side. 'You feel that way because they're your family, and you're emotionally involved. Everyone you know and love is helpless and needy just now, and you're left feeling isolated, as though everything depends on you. It'll pass, believe me.'

'Do you think so? I'm so glad that you were here. I don't know how I would have managed on my own.'

He put his arms around her in a gesture of comfort. 'You would have managed perfectly well. You're as focused as the next person when you need to be, and I expect it was only because I automatically took over that you let me get on with it.'

'I was relieved when you did.' She looked up at him, her eyes troubled. 'Thank you for helping me.'

'I was glad to.' He kissed her gently on the fore-head, smiling softly, and then his expression changed, became more serious, his gaze taking in the contours of her face. He lowered his head and captured her mouth once more, kissing her again, a slow, delicious exploration of her trembling lips.

Allie was helpless in his arms and found herself returning his kiss compulsively, her body suffused with sudden heat, her head whirling with the fog of temptation. She loved the feel of him, the taste of him, the way he was holding her as though she was precious and someone to cherish. It was what she needed, what she longed for, and for the next few minutes all she could think of was how wonderful it was to be held like this, to run her fingers over Nathan's arms, his chest, to feel the warmth of his skin through the light cotton shirt he was wearing, to feel the solid muscularity of his thigh pressed against hers.

Then something changed, and she wasn't sure what it was that made her stop and think about what she was doing. Something was wrong, and she frowned and tried to ease away from him.

'Are you all right?' Nathan looked into her eyes, and she saw that his were still smoky with desire. 'Come back to me.'

'I can't… I…I think I hear Matty calling me… Or maybe it's Owen.' Then she felt something tugging at her heel and she realised what it was that had disturbed her.

'Benjy, stop that,' she said, turning her head and looking down at the puppy. 'Leave my shoes alone.'

He cocked his silky head to one side, as though he was trying to understand what she was saying, and then turned his attention to the hem of her jeans instead.

'No,' she said, more firmly this time.

Nathan chuckled and released her, bending down to scoop the puppy up into his hands. 'He's a lively little thing, isn't he?'

She nodded, still bemused by the way she had fallen into Nathan's arms and instantly lost track of everything. 'Almost too lively sometimes. I can scarcely keep up with him.'

She scanned Nathan's features. He was relaxed and smiling, and that was the total opposite of how she felt. One look from him, the lightest touch, and all her inhibitions melted away as though nothing in the world mattered but being in his arms. What on earth was the matter with her? If it hadn't been for the puppy she might still be kissing him now, and all her good sense would have flown out of the window.

'I'll watch him while you go and see to Matty, if you want.' He was studying her cautiously, as though he had some idea of what she was thinking, and that only served to make matters worse.

'Thanks.' She guessed her colour was high. She could feel the heat of it burning her cheeks, and she turned and fled along the hallway as though her life depended on it.

Matty was fine. He was mumbling in his sleep and had tangled himself in his duvet, so she smoothed it back into place and made sure that he was comfortable once more. He drifted back into deep sleep, his mouth softening, his hands lightly curled at either side of his head.

Allie kissed him and crept out of his room, taking

time to compose herself before she went back to the kitchen.

Nathan was playing with the puppy, throwing a kitchen roll tube for him and then tussling with him for it when Benjy retrieved it.

'Was he awake?' he asked.

'No, just having a vivid dream, I think. He's settled down now.'

'Good.' He looked at her, his lips parting as though he was about to say something more, but then Owen's voice reached them from the dining room.

He was muttering, incoherently at first, and Allie hurried over to him, wanting to reassure herself that he was all right.

'Can you hear me, Owen?' she asked, and he stirred and made an effort to open his eyes.

'Going to court,' he said, his voice slurred, and Allie shook her head.

'No, Owen. You're at home. Everything's all right. You've had too much to drink, that's all. You're going to be fine.'

Nathan came to stand beside her. 'How are you feeling now, Owen? Is your head aching?'

'Head hurts.' Owen frowned, his eyes half-closed as though it pained him to open them. 'Going to court,' he said again. 'They'll put me away.'

'No, they won't.' Allie's tone was sharp. 'I'm sure it won't come to that.'

He opened his eyes and looked at her. 'Tapes,' he said. 'Me in the car.' Then he shook his head as though he was trying to clear it, and winced. 'Not me. They'll put me away.'

'It isn't going to happen,' Allie told him again. 'Jack will come up with something.'

Owen tried a smile, but his mouth wasn't working properly and the whole effect was lopsided. 'Jack's sweet on you.'

'He'll help you.'

Owen's mouth widened. 'Yeah. He's sweet on you.'

Nathan moved away from them and went into the kitchen. He came back a moment later with a glass of water, and held it to Owen's lips. 'Drink this,' he ordered, cupping Owen's hand around the glass and keeping his own hand there at the same time to support it. 'It will help to sober you up.'

Owen drank thirstily, and blinked when Nathan put the empty glass down on to the table. Matty's jigsaw puzzle was next to the tumbler and Allie watched as her brother tried to focus on it.

'Can't leave Matty,' he said.

'You're not going to leave him,' Allie muttered. 'I'll get you some more water, then you might be able to think more clearly.'

'Matty's going to be fine,' Nathan told him. 'You don't need to worry about him. All you have to do is sober up, and then you can help Allie look after him.'

Owen shook his head. 'Bad heart,' he said, then blinked again and focused on Nathan. 'Matty's got a bad heart.'

Nathan took a step backwards, as though Owen had hit him. He shot a look at Allie, but she leaned over and pressed a glass of cold water against her brother's lips.

'Drink,' she said. Why couldn't he have stayed

asleep until Nathan had gone from the house? Now Nathan was sure to start asking questions, and she would have to tell him the truth about what was wrong with Matty when that was something she would have preferred to keep to herself.

Owen finished off the water and closed his eyes, and Allie took the glass back into the kitchen.

Nathan followed her there. 'Is it true, what he said?' he asked. 'Does your son have a heart problem?'

She nodded. 'He was born with several heart defects. His circulation is compromised, and that makes him tire easily. Infections make things much worse for him.'

'I thought he looked pale and a bit blue round the lips. I put it down to the infection, but there's obviously much more to it than that. Can anything be done for him?'

'He'll need an operation at some point, but he's not strong enough for that yet, and there are risks with any surgery, as you know.'

He stared at her in disbelief. 'I don't understand why you didn't tell me any of this before. You've had all that worry to cope with… It wasn't just that you have a child, but he's ill as well, and yet still you didn't confide in me. Did you think I wouldn't support you through that?'

She bypassed the truth. 'Like I said before, I was worried about my job. I thought it might jeopardise things if people knew that I had a son who was ill,' she confessed. 'I wasn't sure how people would react, and I know you've always expected everyone to pull their weight at work.'

'How do you manage?' he said. 'How do you cope, day by day? It must be a tremendous weight on your shoulders.'

'I manage the way I've always done,' she answered simply. 'I take each day as it comes and I get on with it.'

He shook his head. 'I don't think I could brush it aside so easily, but then perhaps by their very nature women are better at handling these situations. I suppose most women are born nurturers, aren't they?'

'I imagine some are.' She looked at him steadily. 'There must be men who would cope just as well.'

'I don't know about that. I know Adam has never come to terms with Dylan's illness, and Megan has always blamed herself for being a carrier. How do you live with something like that?'

She hadn't really expected his reaction to be any different. 'Perhaps *you* couldn't,' she said. 'Other people simply accept what happens and learn to live with it. As for me, Matty is my life. I hurt when he hurts, and I worry about him every day, but the plain fact is he's my son, and I love him. I'll always be there for him and I'll do my very best for him.'

'A mother's love is everything, isn't it?' Nathan gave a wry smile. 'It's good that he has you to care for him. You've always been strong-minded, someone who gets on with things. For myself, I've always had something to aim for, something I've set my sights on. I'm not sure I could have accepted the need to put my life on hold the way you have.'

'Sometimes we have no other choice,' she murmured. She straightened her shoulders. He wasn't going to change, and she had already made her decisions about Matty and they didn't involve Nathan being part of his life. From the way he was speaking now it seemed that it was just as well she had accepted that.

'I know you didn't come here to get yourself embroiled in my problems,' she said, 'but I was glad of your help with Owen. I'll come back to work as soon as everyone's back on their feet. I don't expect to take too much time off, especially once my mother's well again.'

He grimaced. 'It seems to me that's the least of your worries,' he muttered. 'Take all the time you need. I'll try and get cover for you as long as I know what's happening.'

He glanced around, and there was something in his expression that troubled her. She couldn't pin it down, but it was a reflection of emptiness inside maybe, a recognition that all this was alien to him. 'Will you manage all right if I leave now? Do you want me to help get Owen to his room before I go?'

'We'll get by well enough,' she said. 'I'll probably just cover him with a blanket and let him stay where he is.'

'If you're sure?' He glanced at his watch. 'I'm expected somewhere else and I'm late already.'

She nodded and he started towards the hall, distancing himself from everything around him.

Showing him out of the door, she watched him go to his car and start the engine, and as he drove away her stomach knotted. It felt as though something had changed irrevocably and he was going out of her life for ever. Perhaps it was just that her last remnant of hope had died.

CHAPTER SIX

THE boy was shivering, but there was perspiration on his brow and his skin felt clammy to the touch. 'My head hurts,' he said unhappily, and Allie could see that his teeth were chattering.

'How long have you been feeling like this, Jason?' she asked.

'A couple of days.' The ten-year-old had been brought into hospital by ambulance, and Allie was at a loss to know what was wrong with him. His condition wasn't something she had come across before in A&E, and she decided she had to get some test results, quickly.

She had come in to work early because she was supposed to be going out with the search-and-rescue helicopter within the hour, but they were short-handed in the department until the shift changeover and she had stopped to help out.

It wasn't the best of situations to be in. If she couldn't come up with a result fairly soon, she would have to hand her patient over to someone else.

'You're frowning,' Nathan said, coming to stand beside her as she studied the boy's chart. 'Is there something you can't sort out? You have to be out of here soon, don't you?'

She grimaced. She might have known that he wouldn't miss anything. Glancing up at him, she saw that he had abandoned his jacket and was dressed more informally today in chinos and shirt. He looked good but she tried not to dwell on that.

He often left off the jacket when there were children around, because he felt it was much less intimidating for them. That was something she had noticed about him...he was always friendly and caring in his manner with youngsters, and it was such a contrast from the way he'd behaved towards her of late. That disturbed her.

These last few days he had seemed to be cautious around her, withdrawing from her ever since he'd discovered that she had a child with problems. Was he simply concerned because she hadn't confided in him? Or was there more to it than that? Either way, it bothered her that he was treating her with straightforward courtesy, as though they were simply two professionals doing their jobs.

Allie said slowly, 'I'm not sure what to make of this case. He was brought in because he began to have convulsions, and his GP put them down to feverishness. He's generally unwell, and he has a headache and he's been vomiting. From his symptoms it could be influenza, but I'm doing tests for hepatitis, just the same.'

'Has he been out of the country recently?'

She was startled for a moment. 'I don't know. That hadn't occurred to me... It's a little early in the season yet, I would have thought, but I'll have a word with his parents about that.'

'It might be as well. If he's been travelling anywhere in the tropics with them, it could be that he's picked up a bug or a parasitic infection.'

'Like malaria, you mean?'

'That's a possibility.'

'But surely they would have taken preventative measures before going?'

'Even so, if they left it too late, or he lapsed and missed a few doses of medication, he might have fallen prey to an infection. Check up, and then do a blood film and urine tests.'

She went and did as he suggested, and then went to grab a coffee from the doctors' lounge. The results wouldn't be back for a while, but at least she had set things in motion before handing over to a colleague.

Nathan put his head round the door a few minutes later. 'The copter's here. Are you ready?'

'I'm all set.'

'Come on, then. Let's go.'

'You're coming with me?' She hadn't expected that.

'Is that going to be a problem for you?' He was looking at her through narrowed eyes, and she hurried to deny it.

'No…just the opposite, really. I wasn't sure that I'd be able to do this on my own. It's quite a load to take on, having to deal with the unexpected in out-of-the-way places. Around here, everything's so organised that I feel I can do my job without worrying too much. Out there is going to be quite different.'

'I'm sure you'll cope. You seem to adapt pretty well to most things that come your way.'

It was good to know that he had confidence in her, but she hoped that would be enough to get them through the day. It was going to be difficult having him in such close proximity for the next few hours.

Pushing her doubts to one side, she followed him to the helipad.

Their first callout was to a road accident, off the beaten track, where the patient needed an urgent airlift to hospital. His condition was desperate and called for immediate surgery, and if he had to wait for the ambulance to get there by road he wouldn't survive. As it was, they rushed him to Theatre just in time.

The hours seemed to flash by. Working with the search-and-rescue team was so different that she forgot her worries, and it was mid-afternoon before Allie realised it.

'Where are we heading off to now?' Nathan asked the pilot as they prepared for take-off once more.

'This is our last call of the day before changeover,' the pilot answered. 'The paramedics on the ground have asked us to go and pick up a man who's had a fall in one of the valleys. He was out for a walk and fractured an ankle. I'm not sure how they knew where to find him, but the ambulance can't get down there.'

A short time later they were circling above a ravine, and the pilot was looking for a safe place to land. 'This should do us,' he said after a while. 'It's as close as I can get.'

'There he is,' Nathan said, as they scrambled out onto a grassy area a moment later. He pointed to where the paramedics waited, and Allie saw that an elderly man was lying on a stretcher.

A dog was waiting patiently by his side, and she said quietly, 'I wonder if that's how they found him...through his dog?' As they moved towards him, though, things seemed to be going wrong, and as though he sensed it the dog started to whine.

'His heart's stopped,' the paramedic said. 'We had to defibrillate him, but now he's arrested again. We've shocked him three times, but he's not responding.'

Nathan acted quickly. 'I'll give him a shot of adrenaline,' he said, and Allie moved in to help with CPR.

'I've got a pulse,' she said after a minute or two and further defibrillation. Relieved, they stabilised their patient and transferred him to the helicopter.

'We've been in touch with his family,' the paramedic said. 'They're on their way to the hospital now.'

'What are we going to do about the dog?' Allie asked. It was clear that the man was unhappy at the thought of being parted from him. 'Could we take him with us?'

Nathan frowned. 'I suppose we could, if Dave doesn't object.' He glanced towards the pilot, who grinned and nodded.

'Looks like he's not planning on being left behind, anyway,' he said, watching the dog resist the paramedic's attempts to hold him back.

Nathan's mouth indented as he sent Allie a quick look. 'Do you think you could hold him still while I see to the patient?'

She nodded. 'I can manage that, but I don't know what we're going to do with him when we get to the hospital. We'll have to wait for a relative to come and collect him, I expect.'

Luckily, the man's daughter was waiting for him

when they arrived at the emergency room. 'Is my father going to be all right?' she asked anxiously.

'He should be,' Nathan told her. 'He seemed comforted to have his dog stay with him, and I think that must have helped him to keep a grip on things. We'll sort out his ankle fracture and admit him for observation.'

He went with the woman to see to it that their patient was comfortable, and Allie went to sort out a few loose ends.

When she came back to the desk a short time later, Nathan was free once more. 'You're still here?' he commented. 'I thought you'd finished for the day.'

'Not quite. I went to check up on my patient from this morning. Jason Davies…do you remember?'

'I do. How is he?'

'He's not doing too badly. It was malaria, as you suspected. The family had been on a trekking holiday, and they hadn't realised that he might not be fully covered by the time they arrived at their holiday base. I've referred him to the infectious diseases unit for treatment and follow-up. With any luck we'll have caught this at an early stage and he should come through it all right.'

'That was a good result.'

She sent him a quick look. 'It was all down to you. It hadn't occurred to me that he could have a parasitic infection.'

'Put it down to experience.' He gave a wry smile. 'I've been working in A&E for quite a bit longer than you after all.'

'That's true. You had a head start on me.' She gave

him an answering smile, and for a moment he held her gaze, long enough for a little glow of warmth to start up in her. They had been together all day, and this was the first time she had felt a true affinity with him.

'You did well today,' he murmured, 'for all that you were worried about it to begin with. You got on with things and you were confident in what you were doing.'

'I'm glad it seemed that way. I have to feel my way and hope that I'm doing the right thing, but I was glad that you were there with me. I trust your judgement.'

He smiled, his blue eyes scanning her briefly. 'You were fine. Are you off home now?'

'No, not yet. My mother's bringing Matty in to the hospital. He has a check-up this afternoon. It's a late appointment, because the doctor's fitting him in at the end of his session.' She looked at him warily, half expecting him to stiffen and back away, but he didn't.

'Is she bringing him here, to meet you in A&E?'

'Yes. She should be here any time now.'

'I'd like to see her—to talk to her when she comes in. It's been so long since I saw her last.' He glanced at her. 'I didn't get to see much of Matty either. He was tired and unwell and you whisked him off to bed. Perhaps I'll be able to meet him at the same time?'

'Yes, of course. If that's what you want.' She was surprised by the request, because up to now she had thought he might be trying to distance himself from her, but at the same time she was pleased that he wanted to meet her family.

When her mother came in just a short time later, her face lit up as she recognised him.

'I've been hoping that I would see you again,' she said. 'I was so annoyed with myself for being ill when Allie told me you had visited and I'd not been able to talk to you. How are you? What have you been doing with yourself these last few years?' She half turned and drew Matty forward. 'You haven't had much of a chance to meet my little grandson, have you?'

Allie had warned her not to say anything more if she should bump into Nathan today, and her mother was being circumspect. Even so, she put her hands on Matty's shoulders and showed him to Nathan.

Matty tilted his head slightly to one side and looked back at him. It was a characteristic gesture, and one that was uncomfortably similar to the way Nathan often reacted when meeting new people.

'I seed you afore,' Matty said. 'You was at my house.'

'So I was.' Nathan hunkered down in front of him, bringing himself to Matty's level so that they had better eye contact. 'You were feeling a bit poorly, though, weren't you? Are you a little bit better now?'

Matty nodded solemnly. 'Me got new racing car,' he announced. 'It goes faster 'an fast. It's well good. You want to see it?'

Nathan laughed agreement. 'Yes, I do.'

With a triumphant flourish, Matty produced the bright red racing car from his trouser pocket and scrambled down on all fours. 'See—this is what you do…'

He pushed the wheels down on the floor and sent the car whizzing into the wall.

'That is definitely well good,' Nathan said, his eyes wide with appreciation. 'Formula One at the very least.'

Matty beamed, retrieving the car.

'It was a present,' Allie explained in a low voice. 'Jack bought it for him to cheer him up after his latest bout of illness. He thought it would be something to take his mind off coming to see the surgeon today.'

Nathan's eyes darkened. 'Is Jack his father?' he asked.

Allie shook her head. 'No.' The word caught in her throat, and she was glad that her mother was distracted for the moment, watching Matty. 'I told you, his father didn't stay around.'

'It's hard for me to get my head around that. You've always been so sensible, so careful and in charge of your life. I can't imagine how you would let yourself get tangled in a relationship that appears to have been so casual.'

'We all make mistakes.' She went and took Matty by the hand. 'We should go and show your car to Mr Lewis,' she said. 'I bet he'll think it's wonderful, too.' Glancing at her mother, she asked, 'Are you going to stay here and talk to Nathan for a while?'

Her mother nodded. 'As long as he's not too busy.' She sent him a querying glance.

'Not at all. I was just going on a break. Come through to the doctors' lounge and we can talk there.'

Allie sent her mother a look from under her eyelashes, hoping against hope that she wouldn't give away any of her secrets. Her mother smiled sweetly in response.

'I'll meet up with you and Matty later,' she said.

Allie took Matty over to the cardiology department. She was worried about the forthcoming session with the specialist surgeon, not knowing whether he would be able to give her a date for Matty's operation, or whether he would hold out any hope that his condition would improve.

'There's an element of risk with any surgery,' he said, 'but I don't think we can leave things as they are for much longer. This latest bout of infection has taken a lot out of him.' He glanced at her, looking for her acquiescence, and she nodded.

He checked his waiting list. 'We'll book a provisional time for him to come in for the operation for a few weeks' time, and hope that he's strong enough by then to undergo the procedure.'

When Allie went to find her mother she was feeling subdued. She had known for a long time that the day of Matty's operation was coming. Part of her welcomed it, and the chance that he would make a full recovery and have the opportunity of growing strong like other children, but part of her was apprehensive about how things would turn out.

'All done?' her mother said in greeting. She gave Matty a hug. 'Let's get you home, chick. I've made apple pie for supper. You'll like that, won't you?'

Matty nodded. 'Where dat man?' he asked.

'He's a busy doctor, like your mother, and he's looking after a patient.'

They walked out to the car park, and Allie and her mother exchanged glances.

'Have you got a date for the operation?' her mother asked.

'Yes. The surgeon thought it should be sooner rather than later. It was what I expected, really.' She sent her mother a quick glance, and said in an undertone, 'How did you get on with Nathan? You didn't tell him anything about Matty, did you?'

'Of course I didn't. You can trust me...even though I think you're wrong in keeping it from him. Matty's his child and he should know the truth.' Her mother smiled. 'He's taking us all out to dinner at the weekend, by the way. I accepted on your behalf, so I hope you won't try wriggling out of it. Owen's invited as well. I'll have a word with him about it when we get home.'

'Why would he want to take us out?' Allie gave her mother a suspicious glance. 'What have you been up to?'

'Nothing at all. He said it was to thank me for being a good friend when he was younger, and that he would like to show us around his new house.'

'You asked him, didn't you?'

Her mother was affronted. 'I wouldn't dream of doing such a thing. I just said that I'd love to see his home and he offered. He said we'd go to dinner first and then back to his place. He thought Matty might enjoy the garden, so there you are. And you can't get out of it because Matty won't go anywhere new without you going along with him. There are swings, apparently, which the previous owners left behind, and a slide. He kept them because he thought Dylan might like to play on them when he visits.'

Her mother had it all sewn up, and Allie wasn't sure how she felt about that. It was one thing seeing Nathan at work, but anywhere else was a different matter. Things could never go back to how they had been years ago. So much had changed for both of them, and now she had Matty to think of.

Nathan called for them as arranged on Sunday, which turned out to be a glorious early summer's day.

'I'll follow you in my car with Matty,' Allie said. 'He sometimes gets a little carsick, and I wouldn't want there to be any accidents on your beautiful up-holstery.'

'That doesn't matter. We can all go together.'

'I'd rather not. I prefer to do it this way, just in case I have to leave early with him. I'm not sure how he'll react to being out for any length of time. Besides, his child seat is in place and it would be fiddly to remove it.'

He frowned, but accepted that was what she wanted to do, and they set off, her mother and Owen in his car, with Allie and Matty following in hers.

They had dinner at a beautiful country pub where there were landscaped gardens and a play area for Matty.

'Will he be all right climbing up there, do you think?' Nathan asked, as they watched the boy run towards a construction that looked like a tree but had doors and windows and a lookout area on top.

'I think so,' Allie said. 'I'll keep an eye on him,

and distract him if he gets tired. He only gets frustrated if I try to stop him, and usually he knows his own limitations.' Already Matty had made some friends out here, and it was good to see him laughing and having fun.

She put up a hand to shield her eyes from the sun as she watched him play. She was wearing a linen skirt and a sleeveless cotton top, and the sun was warming her skin. Despite her misgivings about coming, she was beginning to relax and enjoy the day out. Her mother and Owen were sitting at a bench table on the lawn, sipping at cold drinks, and they looked as though they were having a good time, too.

'Thank you for the meal,' she said, glancing at Nathan. 'It was delicious, and it's been good to come out here and forget about work for a while. I'm sorry if my mother put you up to it.'

'She didn't. I wanted to spend some time with her and Owen. It's been a while since I've seen them. I thought it would do you good to get away, too. You've had a lot on your plate these last few years.'

'I had the feeling that you thought I'd brought some of that down on my own head.'

He looked at her in surprise. 'Why would you think that?'

'From what you said before about casual relationships… I thought you were judging me and finding me wanting.'

'Perhaps I know you better than you think. I know that isn't what you would want.' He studied her. 'I do get the feeling that something's not quite right, that there's something you're keeping from me. You've changed over these last few years. We've always been more than just friends, but since we've been working together you've been shutting me out. I wasn't altogether sure why.'

She winced. 'I wasn't certain that you would want anything to do with me outside work. You're my boss, and you have to keep a professional slant on things in the department. And, if we're being honest, you seemed to be put off when you learned that I had a child.'

'I was taken aback, more than anything else. I hadn't expected anything like that and it took me a while to get used to it. It doesn't mean I think any less of you.'

'I'm glad.' Her mouth relaxed into a smile. 'It's been difficult these last few months, getting to know you all over again. I felt as though I was on the wrong foot all the time.'

He looked at her quizzically, but he must have had second thoughts about delving any deeper. 'We'll put all that behind us, shall we? Come and see my house. I've only been in there a short time, so it still needs a bit of work to get it the way I want it. I'm pleased with it, though, and I thought Matty might enjoy seeing the garden. He seems to have had a hard time of it, but he's a plucky little chap, isn't he?'

'Yes, he is.'

Nathan had been gentle and understanding in the way he treated her, and she was almost tempted to tell him the truth, but things had been fragile between them lately and she thought better of it.

At his house, a while later, she was impressed. 'It's

not what I expected,' she confessed, after he had shown them around. 'It's big, and beautifully laid out, and the views are stunning. I've become so used to living on one level that I'd forgotten what it's like to look out over such a landscape, and to be able to do it from that balcony terrace must be a joy.'

'It is, especially on a lovely warm day like today.' He smiled. 'I think, for Matty's sake, we had better go out into the garden, though. I'll fix us some cool drinks.'

The garden was massive, with lush green lawns and curved flower borders and nooks and crannies hidden by trellised areas and pergolas festooned with climbing plants.

Matty was in his element. 'Wow,' he said. 'Look, Owen. Pond wiv fishes.'

'Don't go too close,' Allie warned.

'I'll look after him,' Owen said, taking his hand. 'Anyway, there's a little ornamental fence around it, so he can't get too near.'

'Come and sit down,' Nathan suggested, leading Allie and her mother over to a table on the patio. 'You can tell me what's been going on in your neck of the woods.'

They chatted for a while, and then her mother asked about the search-and-rescue work they were doing. 'It must be an amazing experience,' she said. 'Allie said there was a man who had been injured, and he had been lying there for some time while his dog had gone for help. He must have been very lucky.'

'The paramedics told us that the dog ran up to another walker and kept going backwards and forwards until he finally followed him and saw what had happened. After that the dog stayed by his master's side and wouldn't budge.'

'There's no one more faithful than a good dog,' her mother said. 'I think that's why Owen is so glad to have our Benjy.'

'Has he heard any more about his court appearance?' Nathan asked. 'Is it still going ahead?'

Allie shook her head. 'Jack was hoping he would find evidence to clear him before it reached court, but he's having trouble doing that. Apparently, there were two youths involved in stealing the car, and they both ran away. The police got hold of one youth and he said he had nothing to do with the theft and gave Owen's name and address instead of his own. So now they think they have the right suspect.'

'They can't go on supposition, surely? How can they be so sure the one they found is telling the truth?'

Allie's mother said flatly, 'They found Owen's fingerprints on the car, but he says he just looked at it when they showed him, and then he left them and had nothing more to do with it. He said he didn't want to get into trouble.'

'I didn't do it,' Owen muttered, coming over to the table. 'I wasn't with them when they stole the car. I was in the town hall square, talking to a friend, when it was supposed to have happened. I wasn't going far away because Allie was due to pick me up a bit later. Not that the police will listen.'

Allie glanced across the garden and saw that Matty was playing on the swing. 'We believe you,' she said.

A shadow cut across them, and she looked up to

see that someone else had joined them in the garden. She blinked, recognising Nathan's father. He was tall, as she remembered, and broad-shouldered, very much like an older version of his son, though his hair was greying a little at the temples.

He nodded towards her in a gesture of acknowledgement, and then to her mother and Owen.

'I thought I heard voices, so I came around the back,' he said, looking at Nathan. 'I rang earlier, and you were out, but I guessed you would be home round about now. I was passing and I saw your car, so I thought I'd drop in and perhaps have a word with you about Dylan. I didn't mean to interrupt anything.'

'That's all right.' Nathan glanced around the table and then back towards his father. 'Sit down and have a drink with us. You remember Gwyneth and her family, don't you?'

'I do.' He gave an awkward smile, but didn't accept the invitation to sit. Instead, his gaze travelled over the small group gathered at the table. 'It must be a few years since we last met. I hope you're all well—especially you, Gwyneth. I know you had a bad time of it a few years ago.'

'I'm fine, thank you.'

Matty jumped down off the swing to come and stand next to his grandmother, and Nathan's father looked startled. 'I didn't realise there was an addition to the family.'

'He's my son, Matty,' Allie said.

'I had no idea that you had a child.' He looked at her as though he was taken aback by the news.

'What's your name?' Matty asked. 'Is you a doctor as well?'

Nathan's father shook his head and moved a step closer to him. 'I'm not a doctor, I'm afraid, and I don't actually go out to work any more.' He smiled. 'My name's Ethan.'

Wide-eyed, Matty looked up at him and then retreated behind Allie as though he was unsure of himself.

'Have I said something wrong?' Ethan looked a trifle confused, and Allie reflected wryly on how unusual it was to see him react that way.

Owen said softly, 'I think he's anxious because he doesn't know you and you seem to tower above him.'

'Oh, I see. I wasn't thinking… I didn't realise that.' Ethan pulled out a chair and sat down, looking uncomfortable. After a moment or two, he glanced at Owen. 'I couldn't help overhearing that you're in trouble again. I'm sorry about that.'

'It wasn't my fault,' Owen said defensively.

'No?' It was part statement, part question. 'From the sound of things you've got yourself in with a bad crowd again.' Ethan frowned. 'Perhaps you should be more careful how you go about choosing your friends.'

Owen's mouth tightened. 'You sound as though you're still a magistrate,' he said tersely. 'I'm older now. I've changed.'

'Have you? Why don't the police believe that?'

Nathan interrupted quietly, 'Shall we talk about this some other time? Do you want to tell me about Dylan? Has he had another fall?'

Ethan ignored the interruption. He was on his soap-box and warming to his theme. 'The police can only go on the evidence presented to them,' he told Owen. 'If your fingerprints are on the car, it looks bad.'

Owen stood up abruptly, his face taut with anger. 'I don't have to stay and listen to this. I'm not in your court now, and I'm sick of having to say that I didn't do it. People like you never think that people can learn from their mistakes. You're always ready to condemn and criticise.'

'Owen, leave it.' Gwyneth got to her feet, looking shaken. 'I think we should go now. Matty's getting tired and we ought to take him home.' She turned to Nathan. 'Thank you for a lovely day. I really enjoyed it.' Glancing at Allie, she said, 'Would you mind driving us home?'

Allie opened her mouth to answer, but Nathan cut in, his face etched with concern. 'I'm sorry that the afternoon should end this way. Won't you stay for a while longer? You haven't even finished your drink.' When Gwyneth remained standing, he tried again. 'I'm sure nobody meant any harm. It was just a blip from the past, but I'm sure we can get over that. I brought you here, and I'm happy to drive you home a little later.'

'I can take myself home, Mum,' Owen said. 'I didn't mean to upset your day.'

'I think we'll go,' Allie said, getting her things to-gether and taking Matty by the hand. She sent Nathan a quick glance. 'We had a good time this afternoon, but we should leave now.'

As a family, they began to move together towards the side gate.

Nathan went after them, laying a hand lightly on Allie's arm. 'You shouldn't pay any heed to my father,' he said. 'I'm sure things will work out. If Owen's telling the truth, it will all come out in court. There's no need for him to get upset.'

'Well, there's the rub, isn't it?' Her eyes flashed. 'That little word…if. It's such a small word, but it can mean so much.' She pulled her arm away from under his hand. 'I know Owen's done nothing wrong. He shouldn't have to keep trying to prove himself.'

'I didn't mean it that way.'

'Didn't you?' Her voice was drenched with scepticism. 'You'll have to excuse us. We need to go.'

She felt wretched, leaving like that. Afterwards, when they were home and she had put Matty to bed, she sat on the edge of her bed and thought about how it had all gone wrong. It had been such a lovely day to begin with, and she had felt a small surge of hope grow inside her that things might finally start to go right for her and Nathan. Instead, all her newfound happiness had started to crumble around her.

'Allie…' Owen came into her room and she quickly wiped away the dampness from her eyes. 'I'm sorry about what happened,' he said. 'I didn't mean for everything to be spoiled that way. I know you were beginning to get on well with him, weren't you?'

'Don't worry about it,' she said. 'It's not your fault. Ethan was out of line.'

'He was only saying what he thought to be true. Me and my big mouth. It's always getting me into trouble.' He pulled a face. 'I think I'll go out for a walk. I need to be on my own for a bit to sort myself out.' He glanced at her. 'Don't wait up for me. Jamie's working the late shift tonight and I said I'd go round to his house when he finishes. We'll probably watch a video and then crash out.' He studied her anxiously. 'Will you be all right?'

'Of course I will.' She tried on a smile. 'Go and see your friend. It'll do you good to talk to him.'

He left the house a moment or two later, and Allie brushed another tear away from her cheek. Nothing was ever going to go right for her, was it? How could she ever stand a chance of making a go of things with Nathan when his father was so set against her and her family?

CHAPTER SEVEN

'OWEN hasn't come home yet, Allie, and I'm worried about him. He was in such an odd mood last night.'

Allie put Matty's breakfast dishes in the sink and glanced at her mother. 'It's early still. He said he'd probably stay over at Jamie's.'

She wiped Matty's grubby face and sent him to put on his coat for nursery school. 'I wouldn't stress yourself too much. If he hasn't come home by later on this morning, you could always try giving Jamie a call. His number's in our book.'

Gwyneth nodded. 'You're probably right. I'll do that.' Her face brightened. 'You get yourself off to work. I'll see to Matty.' She helped clear the rest of the dishes from the table. 'Are you off in the helicopter again today?'

Allie nodded. 'It's my last trip out with the rescue service. We've each done a few days with them, and it's been an eye-opener, I can tell you. I think we've all come away from it a bit wiser. I never really appreciated how difficult some of the rescue manoeuvres can be.'

'Well, you take care.'

'I will.' She kissed Matty goodbye and gave her mother a hug. 'Let me know if there's any problem with Owen, or with Matty. I'll have to keep my mobile switched off so it doesn't interfere with the equipment, but I can leave you another number that you should be able to reach me on.'

She left for the hospital soon after that, and Nathan met up with her on the helicopter pad. She was busy tying the straps of her medical kit and, apart from acknowledging her briefly, he didn't try making any small talk. His shoulders were braced against the wind-lash from the blades of the incoming helicopter, and even when they climbed inside and were at last airborne he remained silent.

Allie thought she should make the first move. 'Did your father manage to sort out Dylan's problem with you?' she asked, when they had settled into the journey.

'I think so. He wanted to know if there was any kind of padding they could use to protect his knees and elbows. They can't guard against every fall, but they can do something to minimise the chance of injury.'

'I'd have thought Dylan's parents could get that information from the haemophilia centre,' she said, puzzled.

'Under normal circumstances they would, but the staff are in the process of moving to a new building and things are a bit chaotic for the time being. They're coping with the essential matters of care, of course, but other equipment's in transit at the moment.'

'So what's going to happen in the meantime?'

'I've had a word with a specialist at the hospital, and he's given me some samples to pass on. I've left them at the desk for my father to pick up some time today. Adam and Megan are both out at work, so it's easier for him to do that for them.'

He sent her an oblique glance. 'I'm sorry about what happened yesterday. It was a bad way for things to end, but I don't think my father realised he was being bombastic. I didn't mean to upset you either.'

'Perhaps I was being over-sensitive and, anyway, I shouldn't have lashed out at you.' His father had always been able to hit on a raw nerve as far as she was concerned. He often thought he knew best, but she wasn't going to throw that in Nathan's face. It had always been a bone of contention between them, and he was bound to defend his father. She had always loved Nathan, but his father's disapproval of her family hung over her like a black cloud.

'You were worried about Owen, and you wanted to protect him.' He glanced briefly out of the helicopter window at the scenery unfolding below them. 'Is there any other evidence against him, apart from the fingerprints and the youth's testimony?'

'Nothing that will stand up. They tried to say that he must have been on jobs with the gang before, and that he had money from the sale of stolen cars, but they can't prove that.'

'I'm sorry. It's difficult for all of you, I know. I wish there was something I could do.'

'You don't have to do anything. If you tried, you would only be at loggerheads with your father.' She straightened her shoulders, retreating into a defensive shell. 'We'll get by somehow. We've coped on our own before.'

He was silent after that, preoccupied with his own

thoughts, and he didn't make any more offers to help. She guessed he thought she would rebuff him if he tried.

Consequently, things were strained between them for most of the day. They worked together as a team, fighting to save their patients, but in the lull when things were quiet the atmosphere was fraught with an undercurrent of things left unsaid.

'I'm getting an incoming call,' the pilot remarked just after lunchtime, when they were heading towards a gully to find an injured child. He glanced behind him, looking at Allie. 'It's a message from your mother. She says your brother hasn't been home yet and none of his friends have seen him since yesterday afternoon.'

'Oh, no…' Allie felt a cold shiver run through her. 'I was hoping he was with Jamie.'

'Do you think there's any reason to be worried about him?' Nathan asked.

'I'm not sure. It isn't like him to disappear, and he wasn't where he said he would be. My mother must be concerned, or she wouldn't be ringing me at work.' She frowned, her mind working overtime, sifting through everything that had happened of late. 'I know he's unhappy.'

Nathan laid a hand on hers, and that small contact made her feel warm and conscious that she wasn't alone in this. 'Do you have any idea where he would go?'

'No, I don't. He likes to walk when he needs time to think, but he could be anywhere. I just hope he hasn't been out in the open all night.' Her gaze was troubled as she glanced up at him. 'I don't suppose the police will even consider searching for him until he's been gone for a day or so. He's an adult, and they'd say he can take off if he wants.'

'It's probably too soon to start worrying just yet. He'll probably turn up at home this evening and wonder what all the fuss is about.'

'You could be right. I'll phone my mother as soon as we land and tell her I'll look for him once I get home.' It was going to be hard for her to wait, not knowing what was happening, and it must be even worse for her mother. Perhaps Owen had taken it into his head to find a room in a bed and breakfast place for the night, so that he could be alone to think things through. That, at least, would be less worrying.

Allie looked out of the window at the surrounding coastal landscape and tried to turn her mind to her job. 'What's happened to the child we're looking for?' she asked the pilot.

'She's fractured an arm, by all accounts,' Dave answered. 'We had a message through from headquarters to say they received a distress call but they can't reach her because of the terrain.'

'Is she alone?'

'Yes, it looks that way. She was probably out walking along the clifftop and managed to slip somehow. There are warning signs, usually, but kids don't always take any notice of them. I suppose she was bunking off school.'

He looked down, scouring the fields and cliffs below them, and after a minute or two he said, 'I think I can see her. I'll look for a safe place to land.'

Within minutes they had set down on level ground and the paramedics were working out how to reach the girl. They could see her lying crumpled on a ledge just a short distance below the clifftop.

'There's not much room to manoeuvre,' the paramedic said. 'It's going to be difficult to get into that narrow space and secure her.'

'I could probably get in there if you winched me down to her,' Allie murmured. 'I'm thinner and shorter than all of you, and I should be able to reach her.'

Nathan frowned. 'It's too dangerous. There's been a rockfall, and you could lose your footing.'

'I'll be safe enough if you make sure I'm strapped into the right equipment. It isn't too far down. I want to give it a go.'

She looked to the chief paramedic for confirmation, and after a moment's thought he said, 'If you're absolutely sure…'

Nathan cupped her elbows with his hands. 'You don't have to do this.'

'I want to.' She was determined, and nothing he could say would stop her. Time was precious if the girl was badly injured, and they couldn't afford to wait for back-up.

Perhaps he recognised that, because he said, 'I'll be helping to brace the line. If you get into trouble, shout and we'll haul you back up.'

A few minutes later Allie was being locked into a harness, and her medical kit was clipped to her belt. She pulled in a deep breath to steady herself. 'OK, lower me down,' she said.

The girl was conscious and obviously in pain. 'It hurts,' she whimpered, her eyes wide and shocked. 'I fell and I can't get up.'

'We'll make sure that you're safe now,' Allie told her. 'I'm going to examine you as gently as I can to see what the damage is. What's your name?'

'Caitlin.'

Allie checked her over swiftly, and noticed that a silk scarf, probably the child's own, had been tied around her arm in an attempt to stabilise it and keep the wound clean. It was strange, because it must have been practically impossible for Caitlin to do it herself—unless she had been injured before she'd fallen.

'Well, Caitlin, I think what's happened is that you've broken your arm near to the elbow. There's a lot of swelling, and we need to get you to hospital. I want you to try to be very brave for me for a minute or two. Do you think you can do that?'

The child nodded miserably.

'Good girl. I'm going to give you an injection to stop it from hurting, and then I'm going to strap up your arm again to make it more comfortable. As soon as I've done that we'll lift you back up to the top of the cliff. All right?'

The girl nodded again, and Allie worked as quickly as she could, securing her in a harness and signalling to Nathan and the paramedics that she was ready to be lifted up to the top of the cliff.

It was an awkward procedure, but once they reached level ground once more, Allie reported her findings. 'She's suffering from a supracondylar humeral fracture. There's been some blood loss, but not as much as I would have expected. I don't understand how it came about, but there was already a makeshift pressure pad against the wound. It looks like it was made from a wad of tissues wrapped in a ripped piece of cloth. I've given her a painkilling injection and an antibiotic, but she needs oxygen.'

'Leave the rest to us,' Nathan told her, gently squeezing her arms. 'You've done really well, but now you should concentrate on getting your breath back. I'll see if I can find out how the pressure pad came to be there.'

'OK.' The struggle to get back to the clifftop had taken more out of her than she'd expected, and Allie did as he'd suggested, sitting on the grass and recovering from her exertions while they secured Caitlin and transferred her to the helicopter.

Allie was about to get to her feet and follow when she saw that Nathan was coming over to her. He looked worried, and she was immediately on alert.

'What's wrong? Has her condition deteriorated? Did I miss something?'

He shook his head. 'No, it isn't that. The reason her arm had already been stabilised is because someone tried to rescue her. He called in the incident on his mobile phone, but then there was a landslip and he suffered a fall himself.' His expression was grim. 'Allie...I think we've found your brother.'

She stared up at him. 'Owen? You mean Owen was the one who helped her?' She scrambled up and went to the cliff edge, looking down. The rockfall was substantial, covering a wide area at the foot of the cliff, but there was no sign of anyone down there.

She glanced back at him, horror making her eyes grow large. 'Are you saying that my brother is down there?'

He nodded, and fear clutched at her. 'But how can he have survived that? What are we going to do?'

'We're going to look for him now. Will you stay with Caitlin? She's stable for the moment, and there's no immediate urgency as long as we get her to hospital in the next hour.'

'But I have to look for Owen.' Anguish gripped her. 'What if he's badly hurt? I need to be with him—'

'No, you don't.' His voice was firm, stopping her from saying any more. 'You're upset, and it will stop you from thinking clearly. I'll go down after him. I want you to promise me that you'll stay with your patient. Will you do that for me?'

Distress clouded her eyes. 'You won't give up until you've found him? You'll make sure that he's brought back up here?'

'I'll bring him back to you, I promise.' Nathan put his arms around her and then turned her towards the helicopter. 'Go and wait for us there. I won't let you down.'

Allie was numb inside, but she knew that he was right. She was shaking with grief and dread, not knowing what had happened to Owen, and she would be useless when it came to getting down there. She trusted Nathan. She would trust him with her life.

He shrugged into his harness, alongside the paramedics, and Allie couldn't take his gaze off him. All the time she was crying inside for her brother. 'Take care,' she whispered. 'It's a long haul down there. Make sure you come back safely.'

He smiled at her fleetingly, and then started the descent. Allie stood and watched from the door of the helicopter, but when Caitlin murmured she went to her side.

She was comfortable for now, but Allie was fully aware that she needed to get to hospital as soon as possible. Too long a delay and the child's blood supply would be compromised, risking permanent damage to her wrist and fingers.

She talked to Caitlin quietly while she waited for news of her brother, monitoring her pulse and blood pressure and making sure that she had enough oxygen. The waiting seemed endless. She thought of phoning her mother, but she would only be upset, and Allie wouldn't be able to reassure her at this stage. Perhaps it would be better to talk to her when this was all over.

After an eternity, she finally heard sounds of the men coming back, and then Nathan appeared at the helicopter door, looking dirt-smudged and worn.

Ashen-faced, Allie stared at him, her eyes wide and apprehensive. 'Did you find him?'

'Yes. He was under the rockfall. They're bringing him back on the stretcher now.'

'Is he all right?' The words came out as a whisper.

'I think so. He was lucky in that he managed to break his fall with some of the foliage growing out from crevices along the way.'

'But he was under all those rocks...'

'I know, but the bulk of them were small and most of the debris was loose earth. I've examined him, and he has cuts and grazes, some of them fairly deep and needing stitches. He'll probably have a lot of bruises later, but basically he's all right. He was unconscious for a time, and pinned down by the rockfall, so there may be some concussion. We'll need to do an X-ray to be sure there's no head fracture, but miraculously, from the looks of things, he's escaped severe injury.'

She closed her eyes. 'Oh, thank heaven.'

'He's suffering a little from hypothermia, so we need to get his temperature back up. Otherwise, I think after he's been in hospital under observation for a while, he should come out of this all right.'

'I can't believe this is happening.' Tears welled up in Allie's eyes and she blinked them away.

Nathan put his arms around her and held her close. 'Are you OK?'

'Yes.' She mumbled the word against his chest. 'Thank you…thank you for bringing him back to me.'

'I told you that I would.' His lips brushed her forehead in a gentle kiss. 'I would never let you down.'

Reluctantly, he put her away from him as the paramedics brought the stretcher into the medical bay of the helicopter, and Allie cast a quick look over Caitlin before going to sit beside her brother. He wasn't saying very much, but she laid her hand over his throughout the journey back to the hospital.

As soon as they landed, their two patients were rushed into A&E. Nathan went with Caitlin to oversee her treatment, and Allie stayed with Owen until he had been for an X-ray and was pronounced free of any fracture.

He was vomiting, though, and she was worried

about his concussion. 'Let Richard take over from you,' Nathan advised. 'You're too close, and you need to stand back and let others take care of him. Richard's a good man. He'll do the right thing by him.'

She didn't argue with him. She was still shocked after the events of the day, and she didn't trust herself to think clearly.

'We're going to admit him for observation,' Richard said. He was a senior house officer, and she knew he was good at his job. 'Give us a few minutes to get him settled on a ward, and then you and your mother can go and sit with him for a while.'

'Is my mother here?' Allie was startled.

Richard looked at her sympathetically. 'Nathan told me he'd called her and told her what had happened. Perhaps he thought you were too shaken to think of doing it.'

'I'll go and talk to her. Where is she—in the waiting room?'

'That's right.'

Allie gave her brother's hand a squeeze and said softly. 'I'll come and see you on the ward in a little while.'

'Thanks, Allie,' he managed, as Richard wheeled him away. 'I'm sorry to put you through all this.'

Her mother had brought Matty along with her. 'I didn't think I would be back in time to fetch him from nursery school,' she explained. 'I thought it best to bring him here with me.' She looked at Allie with frightened eyes. 'Is Owen all right? Nathan said he had concussion.'

'I think he'll be fine, Mum. I've been with him all

the time. We'll go up and see him in a few minutes. They just need to settle him on the ward. Come through to the doctors' lounge and I'll make us a cup of coffee.'

She picked Matty up and kissed him. 'How are you, sweetheart? You look pale. Have you had your lunch-time medicine?'

He nodded. 'Long time ago.'

Allie frowned and looked at her watch. 'I suppose it was. I seem to have lost track of time this afternoon.'

'I should imagine your shift has ended by now, hasn't it?' Gwyneth asked.

'Yes. That was our last call. Thank goodness we managed to find Owen. He could have been lying out there for hours otherwise.' She gave her mother a faintly worried look. 'I was going to call you as soon as I'd finished treating him. I didn't want to worry you before then.'

Her mother managed a smile. 'I know. Nathan told me you were with him, that you wouldn't leave his side. I knew you would stay with him and that made me feel better.'

They passed by the A&E reception desk on their way to the lounge, and Allie was startled to see Nathan's father there, talking to a nurse. Then she remembered that Nathan had said he would be in to collect the packages for Dylan. She stiffened a little and came to a halt, and Matty squirmed in her arms, looking to see who was at the desk.

'Allie…hello,' Ethan said. He nodded to Gwyneth. 'I had to come in to collect some wadding for Dylan. I wasn't expecting to see either of you here.'

Matty frowned at him. His eyes narrowed and he glowered at Ethan, and something about the jut of his jaw reminded Allie very sharply of Nathan just then. 'You made Owen cross,' he said bluntly. 'You bad man.'

Allie grimaced. Out of the mouths of babes... Then she looked at Ethan and saw that his expression was arrested, that he was staring at Matty in a very odd way. It soon passed, and he recovered himself and said quietly, 'Yes, you're right. I'm sorry about that. I shouldn't have made him cross. It was wrong of me.'

He reached into his pocket and found a wrapped sweet and held it out to Matty. 'These are Dylan's favourites,' he said. 'Would you like to have it...to help me to say sorry?'

Matty looked at the sweet and then at Allie.

'Yes, it's all right. You can take it,' she said.

Matty solemnly accepted the token. 'Fanks,' he said, and then added confidentially, 'We going see Owen now. Him poorly.'

Ethan looked at Allie and her mother. 'I heard something of what happened,' he said awkwardly. 'I feel that I'm in some way to blame. I hope he'll be feeling better soon.'

'I expect he will. Thank you.' Allie excused herself and showed her mother and Matty into the doctors' lounge. She was too upset to stay and talk. It was Ethan's comments that had provoked Owen to lash out, and she guessed Owen was regretting his outburst. He must have taken off because he'd felt the world was against him.

Nathan joined them a short time later. 'We can go

up and see your brother now,' he told Allie. 'He's resting, and the ward sister says we shouldn't stay too long.' He glanced at Gwyneth. 'I hope you don't mind if I come with you and look in on him for a minute or two? I just want to satisfy myself that he's all right.'

'I don't mind. I heard that you were the one who found him, and I wanted to thank you for that. I don't know what I would have done if he was still out there.'

They went up to the ward together, and Nathan held back while Allie and her family talked quietly with Owen for a few minutes.

He was feeling more comfortable now that his wounds had been cleaned and dressed, and he was more talkative than he had been before.

'I didn't mean to put you through any more worry,' he told his mother. 'I couldn't get things right in my head. I thought if I walked for a while it would all sort itself out, but it didn't work out that way. Then it started to rain and I sheltered in an old disused cabin for the night. I fell asleep and started out again in the morning. When I heard the girl crying I went to see what had happened.'

He glanced at Allie. 'Is she all right? They told me she had broken her arm. I tried to do what I could for her, but I wasn't sure I was doing the right thing.'

'She will be,' Allie reassured him. 'You did really well. You kept her arm from moving, and that was the most important thing, as well as stopping the bleeding.'

'I remembered a few things you told me when you were doing your training, but there wasn't much I could use. She had a scarf tied around her waist, over her trousers—a decorative thing, I think. Apart from that, I only had some paper hankies and my shirt.'

'You did exactly the right thing, and it's thanks to you that she's going to be all right. Her bones were manipulated back into position while she was under an anaesthetic, and the doctor said she should be fine in a few weeks. I spoke to her parents in the waiting room a little while ago and they asked me to thank you for what you did.'

He gave her a weak smile and sank back against his pillows. 'I had to help her. I couldn't leave her, could I?'

Nathan came forward and said quietly, 'How do you feel? Are you in any pain?' Allie moved to make room for him at the bedside. She picked up Owen's water jug from the bedside cabinet and went to the sink to fill it.

'I'm all right, but my head hurts and I'm aching all over,' Owen said. 'The nurse told me she'd bring me some tablets in a little while.'

'They should help. I expect your painkilling injection's beginning to wear off now.'

Matty reached up and put his small hand on Owen's brow. 'I make you picture,' he said. 'You be better then.'

'Thanks, Matty,' Owen said with a hint of a smile, and Matty went to badger Gwyneth for some paper and pencils.

'You need to rest for a few days,' Nathan said, 'and then I expect you'll be as right as rain. I just hope you won't take off again without telling anyone. Your mother and Allie were worried sick.'

'I had a lot to think about. I don't know how things are going to work out, and I keep going over and over it in my head. No one believes in me because of the trouble I was in before.'

'Your mother and Allie believe in you, despite everything that's happened in the past. My father was wrong in the way he spoke to you, but he had a point about the people you mix with. If you were more careful about that, things might start to get better for you, and Allie and your mother would have less to worry about.' He frowned. 'It's all about taking responsibility for your actions.'

Owen gave a strangled laugh. 'You sound like your father. How can you talk to me about taking responsibility when you've caused Allie the biggest headache of all? Talk about the pot calling the kettle black! Every day I see her with Matty and I know that she shouldn't be struggling to bring him up on her own…but were you there for her?' His mouth made a bitter line. 'Of course you weren't.'

Allie returned with the jug and stared at him in shock. Owen must have realised that he'd put his foot in it again because he winced and closed his eyes briefly.

'I'm sorry,' he said, his cheeks flushing with heat. He glanced up at Nathan, his expression guarded. 'I was talking rubbish. I don't know what I'm saying. Take no notice of me. I'm probably feverish or something.'

Nathan stood up, a line making a deep furrow in his brow as he looked at Allie.

'What did Owen mean?' he said, his voice grim. 'Is he saying that Matty is my son?'

She didn't answer, lost for words. Instead, she carefully set the jug down on the cabinet, giving herself time to consider her response.

'Like he said, he's been through a lot today and he isn't thinking clearly,' she managed at last.

Nathan shook his head. 'I know what he's been through, and I know how it's affected him. He sounded perfectly lucid to me. I want to know the truth, and I'll ask again. Is Matty my son?'

CHAPTER EIGHT

'I'M NOT going to discuss this here,' Allie said with as much dignity as she could muster. For three years she had tried to keep this from Nathan, and now everything had been blown wide open. 'This isn't the time or the place.'

'Isn't it?' Nathan's voice was dangerously controlled, and she could see from the stark lines of his face and the paleness of his features that he was growing angrier with every second that passed.

Her mother stood up and intervened. 'You had better go outside, both of you. Allie's right. You're in a hospital ward and you should respect the fact that people are ill in here.'

Allie glanced at Owen. He was looking mortified, devastated by the awfulness of what he had done. She laid a hand on his shoulder.

'It's all right, Owen,' she said softly. 'I know that you were just reacting to what Nathan said. You've been through a lot, and now you have to rest and get your strength back.'

Without another word, Nathan strode to the door, then turned and flashed Allie a flint-sharp look. 'We'll go outside into the grounds, and you can talk to me there.'

She walked over to him, conscious that witnessing their argument was not going to be good for Owen or her mother. As to Matty, he was busy drawing, his tongue thrust out between his lips as he concentrated, and she hoped that he had missed what had been said.

In case she had any thoughts of demurring once they were outside in the corridor, Nathan added tautly, 'I want an explanation, and I'm not leaving this alone until I have the truth.'

Allie followed him, her heart hammering as though it would break out through her chest wall. This was her worst nightmare, and she had absolutely no idea of how she was going to explain things to him. How could she deny the facts any longer now Owen had blurted it all out?

'I'm waiting,' Nathan said, when they reached a small quadrangle at the back of the hospital. 'Is it true what Owen said? Is Matty my son?'

There was no one else about at this time of the day, and Allie was thankful for that. She passed her tongue lightly over her lips and lowered her head. She couldn't go on denying it.

'Yes, he is,' she said, her words laboured. 'I thought it would be for the best if—'

'If I didn't ever get to know about him?' Nathan finished for her, his voice a tight knot of rage. 'You lied to me when I asked you in the beginning if he was mine.'

'I didn't lie to you…not an outright lie.'

'Oh, I see,' he said, his voice drenched with sarcasm. 'I asked you if there was a possibility Matty was mine and you just thought you would be a little sparing with the truth, is that it?'

'I didn't think things would work out very well if

you learned that he was your child. So much time had passed, and I thought it was too late to change what I'd already started.'

'The original lie, you mean? You were hoping that I would never find out that you had a child at all, and then, when that didn't work, you decided that you would pass him off as someone else's offspring. Why did you do that? What possessed you to keep it from me?'

She pulled in a quick breath to steady her nerves. 'You had gone to work in the north,' she flung back defensively, 'and you weren't likely to be around when he was born. I knew that I would never be able to rely on you to be there for him. My mother was ill with a stroke and I had just bought a house in the south of the country. I had Owen to think about, too. Then I was ill myself with a virus of some sort. Everything was going wrong for me. What was I supposed to do?'

'You were supposed to tell me as soon as you discovered that you were pregnant,' he bit out.

'Why would I have done that? So that you could tell me to terminate the pregnancy because he was going to be born with a heart problem?'

He almost staggered backwards at that, as though she had hit him. 'I would never have done that. How dare you stand there and accuse me of such a thing?' His face was white, his mouth edged with fury.

She had never seen him react this way before, and his anger was beginning to alarm her. It wasn't at all what she had expected.

'You never wanted a child,' she said. 'You made

love to me, but you didn't even think about the consequences.'

'I don't recall you doing much thinking along those lines at the time either,' he said through his teeth, 'so don't give me that. When you knew you were going to have a child you should have told me, and I should have been allowed some part in his life. I had a right to know.'

'You have no rights where Matty is concerned.' She glared at him, her own fury rising. 'Do you really believe I would let him be buffeted between the two of us, never knowing whether he was coming or going? And when it comes down to it the truth of it is you would never have wanted a child who has problems as severe as his. You've always hated the thought that something like that should happen to you.'

'I still should have been told. I should have been able to acknowledge my child and to get used to the fact that he has problems. I should have been given the chance to come to terms with it.'

Her jaw set tight with wrath at that. 'My child isn't something you ''come to terms with''. You have to feel for him instinctively, to love him and care about him, not simply adjust to the situation. He's a wonderful boy, with or without his heart problem, and he deserves a father who loves him and cares totally for him without reservation.'

'I already care about Matty. Now that he's grown used to me he likes me, too, he talks to me, and he comes to me and greets me whenever he sees me. I get on well with him.'

'Getting on well isn't enough,' she slammed back.

'He needs total love and commitment. Nothing less will do.'

Nathan went very still at that. He said slowly, 'Do you really think it's so impossible for me to love him? What kind of monster do you think I am?' He moved towards her, his whole body a sudden threat, and she faltered, taking a step backwards. 'Not only have you denied me my child, you've denied my parents a grandson. He's my flesh and blood and he's part of our family, yet you've kept him from us. I can't believe that you could do something like that.'

Allie faced him, her face pale, her voice ominously quiet. 'Your family has never liked mine. Your father looks down on us, and even now, after all these years, he has the nerve to condemn my brother out of hand. I don't believe he's ever going to be able to love my child.'

Her shoulders stiffened. 'As to you, and your feelings, you've always said to me that you couldn't live with the burden of a child with problems. Don't tell me that I've been wrong in what I did. I love my child, and I'll protect him and go on protecting him with all that I have.'

She pulled in a deep breath and glowered at him, beginning to shake with anger and frustration. 'I've had enough of this. It's getting us nowhere. My brother is ill and I'm going back to him. I'm going to be with my family. They need me.'

She swivelled around and would have walked away, but he shot out a hand and restrained her. 'Don't imagine that this is over,' he warned. 'Whatever you might have thought in the past is no longer relevant. Things are going to change from this moment on. I'm his father, and I have rights, too.'

She tore away from him and put as much distance between them as she was able. He was threatening her, but she didn't know what the threat was, and that frightened her. She hadn't expected him to want his son, and now she was afraid that he would try to take him from her. Could he do that?

Owen was in a bad way when she went back to the ward. His headache had worsened and he was being sick again. Guilt washed over her. Had she brought this on by asking him to keep the truth from Nathan? He had let it slip out and it was her fault, because it had been too much to ask of him. Her deception was beginning to involve everyone around her, and that wasn't fair on any of them.

She would have gone to him, but the nurse ushered her away.

'What's happening?' Allie said, and the nurse took her to one side and tried to calm her down.

'He'll be fine. We're giving him something for the headache and something to stop the sickness, but he needs to rest. He's been through enough today. He's suffered from concussion and shock, as well as mild hypothermia. You must leave him now.'

Allie was beside herself with concern. 'I need to tell him that everything's all right and he mustn't worry.'

'I'll pass the message on,' the nurse said calmly but with firm emphasis, 'and you can tell him yourself tomorrow. For now, visiting time is over.'

Allie could do nothing else but accept defeat, and she went and sought out her mother and Matty. They went home, all of them slightly subdued, and Allie made an effort to push her problems to one side so that she could take care of her child. He was tired and fretful, and she realised that it was way past his bedtime.

'We'll have some supper and I'll read you a story,' she said, sitting in the rocking chair and cuddling him. 'I love you—you know that, don't you? You're so precious to me.'

He rested his head against her chest, snuggling into the crook of her arm, and her mother came and watched them for a moment. 'I'll get supper,' she said. 'You stay there with him. It's been a long day, one way and another.'

Next day, at work, Allie tried to push her troubles to the back of her mind. Owen had been kept in hospital overnight, and she had looked in on him first thing, satisfying herself that he had not suffered a relapse. His condition was improving, and she had been able to sit and talk to him for a short time.

Nathan was off duty for two days, and she was glad that she didn't have to face him again right away. But when he returned to A&E the following week, things were tense between them.

He was cool towards her, and kept his distance, but when she was treating a child who had been brought in suffering from febrile convulsions she became aware that he had come to stand by her side and was observing what she was doing.

She secured the girl's airway and gave her oxygen, and then took blood for testing.

'Her temperature's still dangerously high,' Nathan pointed out.

'I know. I'm giving her paracetamol to bring it down.'

'Do you know what's causing the fever?'

'Not yet. I suspect that it might be encephalitis, but I'm waiting for test results to come through.'

He nodded. 'It could be a cold sore virus that's causing her problems. In that case she'll need intravenous acyclovir.'

'I know. I'm on top of it.'

He walked away and went to check on another patient, and Allie suddenly realised that she had been holding her breath. She released it slowly, and then sucked air back into her lungs to relieve her tension.

She accepted that their relationship could never go back to how it had been before, but it was more difficult than she had imagined, contemplating a life without hope. At the back of her mind she had always yearned for a time when things would be as they had been in those earlier years, when she had grown to love him, and he had been there for her, sharing her hopes and fears. She had dreamed that one day he would love her in return. It had been an illusion, of course.

Their argument had played over and over in her head, but now that she had calmed down she couldn't see any way to put things right.

He felt aggrieved, and probably rightly so, but through it all she had acted out of concern for her son. Nathan would never have been on hand if she had told him the truth before this. He had been moving around from one specialist post to another, building up his career, cementing his qualifications as a consultant. How could he have imagined that he could be a father to Matty?

'I want to talk to you in private,' Nathan said later on, taking her to one side. 'Could we find some time to get together this weekend? We need to work out some way that I can have access to Matty, so that I can explain to him who I am and that I'm going to be there for him from now on. My parents want to see him, too, and I think we should sort this out as soon as possible.'

'I don't think that's a good idea just now,' she answered tautly. 'It will be too upsetting for him to have his routine changed. He's going to have surgery in a couple of weeks' time and I need him to stay calm and unworried. It isn't going to do him any good if you start filling his head with things he needs time to take on board.'

'Hasn't he ever asked any questions about his father? Where he is, or who he might be?'

'No. It hasn't come up. He's very young and he doesn't understand properly about mothers and fathers and family relationships.'

'But he goes to nursery school, and sooner or later he's going to realise that other children have fathers who are on hand and part of their lives, and then he's going to want answers as to why his life is different. Haven't you given any thought to how you will explain things to him?'

'Not really. I thought I would deal with it when the time came.'

He gave her a scornful look. 'I don't believe that you would leave things to chance. You must have some idea of what you were going to tell him.'

Her shoulders lifted. 'I suppose I would have said that his father had been away while he was growing up, working in different parts of the country and building up a career for himself, and that he had never known that he had a son...the truth, really. That after several years with no father in his life I thought it would be upsetting for him to have a stranger come into his world and cause everything he had known to suddenly change.'

His eyes narrowed on her. 'Do you really believe he would have accepted that, not been hurt and let down because his father hadn't been around?'

'It would have been more hurtful for him to know that his father didn't want to care for any child who was suffering from a devastating illness. That was what you always said. You saw the way Dylan was, and how upsetting it was for your brother and his wife to live with that, and you didn't want it for yourself. Would you rather I'd said all that to Matty?'

'I said those things,' he acknowledged, 'but I didn't mean that I wouldn't want my own child if it happened that way. It's heartbreaking to know that your child is ill, and no one would want that to happen to them, but when it does it's something you have to accept and learn to live with. Since I've known Matty I've come to realise what a lovely boy he is, and how much he brightens your life. I would never have rejected him. I feel as though I've missed out on something precious, and I can't believe that you would do such a terrible thing to me as to deny me my own child.'

'I was trying to keep him from being hurt all over again. He's already suffered a lot in his young life and I was afraid he would be miserable if he discovered he had a father who was around but didn't want him. I didn't know you would react this way. I was afraid for him.'

Nathan's mouth made a bitter line. 'You don't know me very well at all, do you? How could you think that way about me? He's my son and he has an illness that's blighting his life, and you imagine that I wouldn't want to know about that? Now you tell me he's going to have an operation and you expect me not to care?'

His blue eyes burned into hers. 'Well, I do care, and I'm going to be there for him, whether you like it or not. I'm going to see him and spend time with him at every opportunity I get, and if you try to stop me I'll make life more difficult for you than you ever realised possible.'

'Nathan, I told you, I can't have him upset right now—not just before his operation. You must know how important it is that he stays calm and unworried.'

'Of course I know that. I'm not going to tell him who I am, and for the moment I'll ask my parents to stay away, but I will see him and get to know him better. I won't let you get in the way of that.'

'All right,' she conceded. 'I'm not going to try to stop you from seeing him, but you have to reassure me that you're not going to disrupt his life. He has enough to deal with on a day-to-day basis, and if I get even a hint that he's upset, or his health goes downhill because he doesn't understand what's going on, I'll put a stop to it. Are you clear on that?'

'I am.' A muscle flicked in his jaw. 'I've already told you that I have his interests at heart. I won't do anything to undermine you as his mother or to cause him to suffer a relapse, but I'm determined to be part of his life.'

They stared at each other, each of them stiff and unyielding, and though Allie felt suddenly drained she tried not to show it. This wasn't how she had wanted things to turn out, with her and Nathan battling it out and Matty caught in between.

She had wanted Nathan to love her, as well as their son, but now it seemed that her dreams had been washed away like rainwater inexorably flowing down a gutter. She felt empty inside.

CHAPTER NINE

'ALL we can do now is wait,' the nurse said. Allie barely heard her. She was still staring at the closed doors of the operating theatre, and the nurse gently turned her and led her away. 'Mr Lewis is an excellent surgeon,' she added, 'one of the best in his field. I'm sure your son is in good hands.'

Allie knew that the nurse was trying to comfort her, but it wasn't working very well. Watching your child being wheeled away to an operating theatre was a horrendous thing to have to go through, and even though she had been able to stroke his hair and kiss him before he'd succumbed to the anaesthetic it wasn't enough and she was crying inside.

'Let's go to the waiting room,' Nathan said. 'We can have some privacy in there.'

She looked up at him, but her eyes were blinded by the sheen of tears and she brushed them away with her fingers and then blinked, trying to focus.

His hand rested lightly on her elbow and he urged her forward. 'This way.'

'I wanted to stay with him.' Matty was undergoing surgery, and her mind couldn't let go. She was desperately afraid for her child.

'I know, but you can't do that.' Nathan had been determined to be here with her, and after the last couple of weeks she hadn't expected otherwise. To his credit, he hadn't pushed anything out of respect for her concerns, and although he had told his parents that Matty was his son, he had kept his word and asked them to stay away for the time being.

He had spent some time with Matty every day, either coming to see him at her house or going with them on visits to the park or the local play centre. At each visit he had made it seem as though he had come to see Allie and her mother, but at the same time he and Matty had got to know each other a little better.

'As the nurse said, all we can do now is wait.' Nathan glanced around the waiting room. 'At least we'll be comfortable in here.'

Allie couldn't recall how she had come to be in the room, but she was aware that the nurse had gone out and left them alone together. Locked into her own nightmare, everything around her faded into insignificance. All she could think of was Matty. Over the last few hours she had prayed constantly that he would come through this operation, that all would be well.

Nathan helped her to sit down on the leather upholstered bench seat and then seated himself just a short distance away from her.

'I know this is hard for you,' he said in a quiet voice, 'but the nurse was right in what she said. Mr Lewis is among the best cardiac surgeons in the country. If anyone can bring Matty through this, he will.'

'He's so small and vulnerable, though, and he was getting more frail as the days went by. I can't bear this. What if something happens while he's under the anaesthetic and things go wrong? I don't know how I could go on...'

'We both know the dangers of surgery, but you have to stay positive, Allie. Matty couldn't have gone on through life with his heart being so damaged. This had to happen. You know that.'

She nodded miserably. 'Yes, I know. I'm sorry... I ought to be stronger than this. I'm a doctor. I know how things work, I know all the procedures, but this is Matty—this is my little boy.'

'I understand what you're going through,' he said quietly. 'I've only known him for a short time, but it's painful for me as well. He's my son, too, and I'd have given anything for it not to have come to this.'

She looked up at him with tear-drenched eyes. He looked as though he was feeling as wretched as she was. 'I'm so sorry, Nathan. I've been selfish in the way I treated you. I didn't realise that at the time. I really did think that I was doing the right thing. I know now that it wasn't the best way to handle it. I should have told you about him from the beginning. Can you forgive me?'

'I think I know why you did it. It was hard for me to take it in at first, but deep down I'm beginning to understand your reasoning. Matty was ill and you needed someone who would be there for him full time and wholeheartedly. You weren't sure that I was capable of that.'

He grimaced. 'I'm sorry that you felt that way, that you couldn't find it in you to believe in me, but I do understand.' He was silent for a moment, but then he added, 'I'm glad that at least I found out the truth in time, so that I could be here for him now. Over these last few weeks I've grown to love him, and it's almost as hard for me as it is for you to sit here and wait for news of the outcome.'

'I'm glad that you're here with me,' she said in a whisper. With all the recriminations that had passed between them lately, she hadn't been prepared for that, but it was true. She had felt so alone in all this, and it was comforting to have him here, a solid, supportive presence in the room. 'This isn't something that I would have wanted to share, but it does help, having you near.'

He came and sat close by her side and put an arm around her. His warmth permeated her thin clothing and his strength reassured her, though she was sure she didn't deserve his compassion. Slowly, her sense of isolation began to melt away. 'Lean on me,' he said. 'We'll get through this together.'

She rested her head against his chest. 'This last couple of weeks has been so difficult,' she said in a choked voice, 'knowing that this time was coming. I didn't know how I would cope.' She dashed away her tears with the back of her hand. 'I feel better knowing that you're going to be staying here with me.'

'I needed to be here,' he murmured, 'for both of you.' He was silent for a moment, and then added, 'It can't have been easy for your mother either. She loves Matty to bits, doesn't she?'

'She does. She's been with him right from the start, and this has been terribly upsetting for her. I know the only reason she held back from coming here with me this morning was because she knew you were going to be here. I think she felt we needed some time alone.'

'That was thoughtful of her. Is she coming in later?'

Allie nodded. 'She's going to bring Owen with her. He couldn't bear the thought of not knowing what was happening.'

'He looks a lot better in himself these days, doesn't he? His cuts have almost healed, and the bruises are disappearing.'

Allie managed a faint smile. 'He said he's thankful for that. If he had to go to court looking as though he'd been in a fight the judge would have taken one look at him and had him marked down as a thug. Then things would have been certain to go downhill.'

'Have there been any more results on that score? Will he be able to produce any evidence to show that he wasn't responsible for the theft?'

She sat up and tried to pull herself together. Nathan let his arm slip away from her.

'There's nothing so far,' she said. 'Jack had the surveillance tapes cleaned up, but it still looks as though it's Owen in the driver's seat. Jack said he was going to plead that the footage is inconclusive, but we can't account for the fingerprints on the car.'

'They were on the outside of the car, weren't they?'

'Yes, because Owen said his friends showed him the car as if it belonged to them. He put his fingers on the door while he looked inside at the dashboard, but then it dawned on him that his mates might have been up to no good. He didn't know how they had come by the car, but he became suspicious and then he backed away. He said his so-called friends drove off and he didn't have any more to do with them, or the car. Apparently it was about an hour later when the police were alerted to the fact that it was stolen and started to give chase. You know the rest. They finally caught up with one of them, but Owen said he was in the town hall square at that time.'

'So there was nothing on the steering-wheel?'

'That's true, but it doesn't prove he wasn't there, or that he wasn't driving, because the police maintain he could have put gloves on when he decided to drive, or wiped them away at the last minute. They can't say that in court, though, because it's supposition.'

Nathan stood up and began to pace the room. 'There is one thing that might stand in his favour.'

'What's that?'

'My father's agreed to help out. I asked him if he would write to the court, giving Owen a good reference. As he's a magistrate from another part of the country it might do some good. His comments would stand for something.'

'But Owen appeared before him. Won't that work against him?'

'Not if it's worded in the right way...to say that he feels Owen has been trying to make something of himself by looking for work, and to tell the court that Owen saved the girl in the cliff fall.'

'Are you sure that your father's agreed to do that?' It wasn't an option that would have occurred to her. 'He doesn't usually have any time for Owen, or for the rest of us come to that. I can't imagine that he will want to help us now.'

Nathan pulled a face. 'I think you're wrong about him. It isn't that he's against you. He usually sees things in a certain way, in black and white, with no shades of grey in between, but he's learning to look at things differently. He was surprised to hear about what Owen did for the girl, and I think he'll do what he can to help. He felt bad about upsetting things when you were all at my house that day.'

'I must say I'm glad if he's had a change of heart.' Allie was still puzzled, though. 'Could his decision to help have something to do with the fact that he knows Matty's your child? Perhaps he feels that we have a connection to your family now, and he doesn't want any slur on the family name?'

Nathan shook his head. 'He knows about Matty, it's true, but I don't think that's what's making him do this. I've spoken to him and tried to make him see things in a different light.'

'You did that before, years ago, but it didn't make a lot of difference.'

His mouth twisted. 'Let's just say that he's older now, and he seems to have mellowed with age. He wants to help in any way he can, and putting in a good word for Owen is least a beginning.'

She frowned. 'A character reference is good, but it may not be enough if the evidence is against Owen.'

'That's true, but I'm working on that. I'm looking into something to see if I can find new evidence.'

Allie got to her feet, gazing at him, her expression wide-eyed. 'What new evidence?'

'I'll tell you about it if it works out. It may not be any use, but it's just an idea I had—something I felt might be worth trying.'

She went over to him and laid a hand lightly on his arm. Looking into his eyes, she said, 'Let me get this straight. Even though you've been angry with me over these last few weeks, you've still been looking at ways to help Owen?'

'I thought the least I could do was try.'

Her hand strayed to his chest and rested there, her fingers trembling a little. 'I thought you hated me, and yet all the time you were doing what you could to help.' She stared up at him. 'I misjudged you very badly, didn't I?'

He ran his hands over her arms. 'It's a little soon to expect results, and it may not come to anything. Don't get your hopes up.'

Her mouth relaxed in a soft smile. 'You're trying. You're doing whatever you can. And that's what counts. I can never thank you enough for that.' She rested her forehead against his chest again and his arms came around her, comforting her, making gentle forays along her spine.

They stayed like that for a minute or two, locked in each other's arms. It felt so right, so perfectly natural, and she felt that with him by her side nothing could ever hurt her again. Except... If anything happened to Matty, what would she do? How could she go on?

She said in a low voice, 'I wish there was some news about Matty. We seem to have been waiting for so long.' She looked up at him, her face suddenly white with fear. 'Do you think he'll be strong enough to get through it? He looked so pale this morning. I didn't want to let him go, but I knew that I had to.'

'You've looked after him well all of his young life, and given him everything he needed to make sure that he was as strong as possible. No one could have done any more.' He put a finger beneath her chin and lifted her face to his. 'There's a good success rate with this operation. You need to remember that.'

'I'll try.'

Behind them, there was the sound of a door opening, and they broke apart, turning to see who was coming in.

Owen and Gwyneth walked into the room, both of them looking anxious. 'Is there any news?' her mother asked, but Allie shook her head.

'He's been in surgery for quite a while, hasn't he?' Owen said. 'Is that usual?'

'It's a long operation.' Nathan put his arms around Gwyneth and gave her a hug. 'Try not to worry. If everything goes well he stands to have a good future ahead of him.'

'I don't really understand what they're doing,' Owen said. 'Allie said something about widening the pulmonary artery and repairing the damaged area of his heart?'

'What happens is that the surgeon will close the defect in the heart and he'll reconstruct tracts so that any obstruction is removed and blood can flow freely to where it's needed.'

'Does that mean he'll be better than he was before? Or will he still struggle for breath?'

'It should help him to make a full recovery. If his heart starts to work better he'll begin to grow and thrive, and after a few months he should be able to cope with activity much better than he did before. It's an operation that's recommended these days for children like Matty.'

'How long will it be before we know how things have gone?' Gwyneth sent Allie an anxious glance.

'Another hour, I should think. He's been in Theatre for quite some time already.'

'I'll go and fetch some coffee to keep us all going,' Nathan offered. 'If I see any of the staff involved along the way, I'll ask for a progress report.'

When he came back into the room a little later he was carrying a tray laden with coffee-cups, sandwiches and doughnuts. He passed them around, and Allie shook her head.

'Thanks, but I'm not hungry. I'll just have the coffee.'

'You should eat something,' he insisted. 'I know you didn't have breakfast, and you need to keep your strength up for Matty's sake. He'll need you to be fighting fit when he comes round.'

'Did you manage to find out anything about what's going on?' she asked in a worried tone.

'Yes. I saw one of the nurses come out of Theatre and she says everything's going to plan. There haven't been any hitches or setbacks, and Mr Lewis is satisfied with progress so far.'

'Thank heaven for that,' Allie said in a breathless voice. Her legs were weak all at once and she sat down.

Nathan thrust a pack of sandwiches her way. 'Eat,' he said.

She did as she was told, taking a small bite of a sandwich and forcing the food down. When Matty came out of surgery she was going to sit with him through the day and through the night. She was going to be there at his side come what may.

Time dragged on. The wait for news seemed endless, but at last the door opened and the surgeon came into the waiting room and sat down beside Allie.

'I'm very pleased with the way everything went,' he said, coming straight to the point. 'Matty's in Recovery now, as we speak, and I'm satisfied that we've made a total correction of his heart defects. He'll need to rest and get his strength back, and that will take time, but you can go and see him just as soon as you like.'

Allie clasped his hands between hers. 'Thank you so much for what you've done,' she said, tears of happiness welling up in her eyes. 'I just can't thank you enough.'

'It was my pleasure,' he said. 'If you want to go with the nurse she'll take you to him, and I'll come along and see him a little later.'

Allie stood up and smiled at her mother and Owen. 'I'm so relieved,' she whispered. She could hear Nathan talking to Mr Lewis, thanking him just as she had done, and a moment later they left the waiting room and went to Matty's bedside.

He looked so fragile, connected to monitors, with drips and tubes here and there, but his face was healthily pink, and when she stroked his cheek with a finger he looked at her drowsily and managed a little smile.

'I've brought you a present,' she said, holding up a soft toy dog, which looked just like Benjy. She tucked the toy into the crook of his arm and he gave her another little smile and drifted back to sleep.

She stayed with him while he slept, and her mother and Owen looked on, the big smiles on their faces saying it all. He had come through the operation safely, and his chances of a complete recovery were good.

Nathan was there the whole time, by her side. Matty woke from time to time and mumbled a few words, but when evening came, and he drifted into a deeper, more restful sleep, Allie went to the bathroom to freshen up and then fetched coffee for Nathan and herself.

Her mother and Owen had decided to go home to make sure that the puppy was all right, but said they would be back in the morning.

Returning to the bedside, Allie was surprised to see that Nathan's parents had joined him there. They stood up as she approached, both of them looking faintly worried, and Nathan's mother said, 'Do you mind if we just look at him for a while? We've been so anxious for him, and we hoped you wouldn't turn us away.'

Allie was shocked by the uncertainty in Abigail's voice. The older woman's face looked drawn, and her grey eyes were troubled.

'Of course I won't turn you away.' All at once Allie felt ashamed for keeping them from their grandson, for putting them through such an ordeal. 'Please, sit down and stay. He's been through a lot, though, and I doubt that he'll wake up again tonight.'

'That's all right.' Abigail managed a shaky smile. She pushed a strand of soft brown hair from her cheek in a nervous gesture and added, 'It's what we expected, but we just wanted to look at him and know that he was on the mend. It was such a shock when Nathan told us how ill he was.' She looked at Allie searchingly. 'He said this operation should make him so much better...do you agree with that?'

Allie sat down next to her. 'I do. I was worried about the outcome, but I knew it had to be done if he was to have any chance in life. He should start to improve from here on.'

'I'm glad for you,' Ethan said. 'I can't imagine how hard it has been for you to watch him grow up, knowing that he was so ill.'

'It's been a worry; I'll admit to that.' She gave him a tentative look. 'It must have come as a shock to you to discover that you have another grandson, and even more so to find out that he has problems, too.'

Ethan hesitated for a moment. 'I was startled at first when I realised that you had a child. But then, when I met him again at the hospital the other day, and he was telling me off, there was something about his expression that made me stop and look again. I think I knew then that he was Nathan's boy.'

Allie stared at him. 'You guessed?'

'He looked so much like him, the way Nathan looked as a child, and his expression was so much the same that I couldn't just dismiss the idea. I went home and told Abigail that I was sure we had another grandchild, even though Nathan hadn't told us about him at that stage.'

Abigail said quietly, 'I'm sorry that the poor little lad has been so ill. We've had all the worry with Dylan, but he's a wonderful boy, and I just know we're going to love Matty every bit as much. If there's anything we can do to help, you only have to ask.'

'Thank you.' Allie was subdued, overwhelmed by their unconditional acceptance of her child, even though she had kept him from them for all this time. 'I know that I should have told you about him before this, but it was difficult for me to decide what to do for the best. I thought I wouldn't be able to handle it if you knew the truth, but I realise that I was wrong. I'm sorry.'

'Bless you…you have nothing to be sorry about.' Abigail put her arms around Allie and hugged her. 'I feel so bad that you've had to go through all this on your own.'

They talked quietly for almost an hour, and then Nathan's parents left to go home. Alone with Nathan, Allie leaned back in her chair and watched over Matty as he slept.

Nathan reached for her hand. 'He looks so peaceful, doesn't he? I think he's going to be all right.'

She nodded. 'I hope so. I'm so relieved that he came through it all.'

Nathan's thumb lightly stroked the back of her hand. 'He deserves to have a decent future, with two parents to care for him…a proper family.' He looked at her searchingly, and added in a soft voice, 'Could we do that for him, do you think? Should we get married and make sure that he has everything he could want?'

Allie's breath caught in her throat. He was saying that he wanted to be there for Matty through thick and thin, to be a proper father to him. Wasn't that what she had always wanted?

Ever since she had first known Nathan she had loved him and wanted to be with him for ever, to have him love her in return. But that wasn't what he was offering, was it? He wanted to marry her for Matty's sake.

It would be good for Matty to be part of a strong family unit, but everything in her rebelled against entering into a marriage where the love was one-sided.

'Allie? What do you say? Will you marry me?'

She swallowed painfully against a lump that swelled in her throat. 'I don't think I can give you an answer to that right away,' she answered in a low voice. 'I think I'm still in shock after going through all this, and I'm not up to making decisions like that just yet.'

She looked up at him. 'I know it seems like the right thing to do, but I need time to get myself together so that I can think more clearly.' She ran the tip of her tongue over her lower lip. 'Would you mind waiting for an answer?'

His features were tense, with stark lines etched along his cheeks, but it might have been the shadows thrown up by the dim lighting in the room that gave that impression. He didn't speak for a moment, and she worried that she had alienated him once again.

Then he said quietly, 'No, I understand. This is a bad time for you. I shouldn't have asked just yet.'

He let go of her hand and didn't say any more after that. He simply watched his son, and his expression was brooding.

The silence between them was uneasy, and as time

went on it grew more strained. Allie wished that there was something that she could do to bridge the gulf that had opened up to threaten their newfound closeness, but it was impossible. Even for Matty's sake she didn't think she could marry Nathan if he didn't love her.

CHAPTER TEN

ALLIE was convinced that she had ruined everything. Over the next few days Nathan seemed remote from her all over again, not saying very much—but he was there to watch over Matty whenever he could.

He went back to work during the daytime, but came to visit Matty every evening, and brought with him anything that he thought Allie and his son might need. Allie had taken time off from A&E to be with Matty.

After a few weeks he was well enough to go home with her. She looked up at the clear blue summer sky and thanked heaven that he had improved so much. He would be able to play out in the warm sunshine and grow stronger day by day.

'Me want see Benjy,' he said excitedly as they arrived at the house. 'Me not seen Benjy long time.'

'He's waiting for you,' Allie said with a smile. 'Owen's taken him for a walk, and now he's in the garden so you can play with him there.'

She watched Matty run outside onto the lawn. Owen swept him up in his arms and hugged him, and then set him down to go and chase after the puppy. Her mother followed him, keeping an eye on both of them.

'He looks so much better, doesn't he?' Owen said, coming over to Allie where she stood on the patio. He was smiling widely, clearly happy with what he saw.

'He does. I'm really pleased with the way he's recovering. We need to be careful with him over the next month or so, but he's definitely on the mend.'

'What's going to happen now? Will he be going back to nursery school?'

'As soon as he feels ready. Mum says she'll look after him when I go back to work, but I'm not planning on doing that for a few days. I want to make sure everything's going well before I do that.'

Owen grimaced. 'I'd like to say that I'll be around to help out, but I don't know how things will go in court. Nathan told me he had come up with something, but he needed to make a few checks first and he wouldn't say what it was.'

Allie was surprised. 'I didn't realise he'd talked to you.'

Owen nodded. 'He came over here a couple of times to ask me about what had happened on the evening when the car was stolen. I told him as much as I could. You were at the hospital with Matty, and he dropped by here after he had finished work.'

He gave her a quick glance. 'I know I've told you this before, but I'm sorry I messed things up for you by blurting everything out about Matty being his son. I thought he was having a go at me, and I took a shot back at him. I wasn't thinking properly. Did I ruin everything for you? I know that he's been a bit reserved around you lately.'

'In the end it was probably better that it all came out.'

'But is he OK with you now about everything?'

'Sort of.' She made a little grimace. 'I made a mess

of it all again, but it's good that he knows about Matty. I suppose at least we can move forward now.'

'You can't make any more of a mess of things than I do. I'm always putting my foot in it and getting things wrong. That's probably why I'm going to court.'

'You've come through a lot, Owen, and I know you're on the right track now. It wasn't easy for you when you were young and Dad left us. You were never quite the same after that, and I always thought maybe I didn't do enough to help you through it. Mum was having a nervous breakdown and I had so many things to cope with back then that perhaps I wasn't there for you as I should have been.'

He shook his head. 'You shouldn't blame yourself. You did everything you could…you were a great sister to me. You've always stood by me.'

He frowned. 'I think when Dad left us I thought I had done something wrong. I thought he had gone because I was no good and he didn't love me, perhaps no one could love me, and then I thought maybe Mum had done something wrong to make him go away. Then she was ill and I went back to thinking it was all down to me. He'd abandoned us because he didn't care about us. I was confused and I felt worthless, and for a long time I took my feelings out on everyone and everything around me.'

Something in Allie's chest flipped over at the thought of a small child going through all that heartache. 'You don't still feel that way, do you?'

'No.' He sent her a crooked smile. 'In the end I

came to the conclusion that he was the loser, and I made up my mind things were going to be different. I suppose I grew up.' He gave an ironic laugh. 'It feels like payback to find myself in trouble again when I was going straight.'

'Things might still work out for you. Did Nathan sound as though he thought things might go well for you in court?'

Owen shrugged. 'It's hard to say. He seemed reasonably positive. In fact, he said he was going to have a word with Jack at his office and then he'd come over and talk to me some more. Then he started asking about the kind of jobs I'd been going after, and what was behind me not getting them. I think he wanted to help me any way he could.'

Allie hadn't realised that Nathan had been so active on Owen's behalf. Perhaps she had been so wrapped up in worrying about Matty that he hadn't wanted to confide in her. 'Did he have any ideas on that score?'

'I think so. He seemed to have something on his mind. He knows I get on well with animals and have a way with them, and he wanted to know if I'd thought about doing any kind of work along those lines. I get the feeling he's looking into things for me. Anyway, he said he knew Matty was coming home today, and he was planning on coming over here to see him when he'd finished work. He said he would talk to me some more then.'

Throughout the rest of the day Allie concentrated on watching over Matty. He had been through such major surgery, and she didn't want him to tire himself out or suffer any kind of setback.

'Where Nathan?' he asked later on in the afternoon.

'He's at work, but he said he would come and have a meal with us later today. You'll be able to see him then.'

Matty seemed to be satisfied with that answer, and turned his attention back to his toys. The front doorbell sounded and Allie heard Owen go to answer it. It was probably her mother, back from the shops and wanting a hand with her packages.

She concentrated on getting things ready for tea, setting the table in the dining room while Matty played with his construction blocks on the floor. He was making a barn for his farm animals, which were dotted about the carpet, enclosed by a makeshift fence of cardboard.

Allie looked at him with affection, wondering how much she ought to tell him about his father. Sooner or later he was going to have to know the truth. She knelt down beside him and said carefully, 'You like Nathan, don't you?'

Matty nodded. 'Him play wiv me.' He trotted a plastic horse into a barn and then frowned. 'When me was poorly him said we make castle.'

'With your blocks?'

Matty nodded again. 'But him not here.' He picked up a toy farmer and sat him on a green and white tractor, making 'brumming' sounds as though he was driving.

'He will be in a little while.'

'Why him not live here, like Owen and Nanna?'

'Would you like that?'

'Yes. Him could be my daddy.' He looked up at

her, his eyes clear and bright. 'My friend at school's got a daddy.'

Allie swallowed hard. 'Matty, sometimes daddies don't live with their children. It would be lovely if they did, but things don't always work out that way.'

He looked up at her from under his lashes. 'But him could be my daddy?'

'Yes, that's true. He could.'

Matty gave her a beaming smile and trotted another horse into the barn.

There was a muffled sound behind them, and Allie looked around to see that Nathan was standing in the doorway, his hand resting on the doorjamb. He was tall and strong, long-limbed, dressed in casual clothes—smart chinos and a linen shirt that was open at the neck to show his lightly bronzed throat. He took her breath away and she floundered for a moment. She had no idea how long he had been standing there.

'I didn't realise you were here,' she said, her lungs choked from lack of air. 'I suppose Owen let you in?'

'Yes, he's just gone to help your mother with her bags. We both arrived here at the same time.'

She stood up, and at the same moment Matty scrambled to his feet and ran over to him. 'Mummy said you was coming. Me made a barn. Come and see.' He took Nathan by the hand and tugged him over to his playthings.

'That's a very good barn,' Nathan said in approval. He knelt down to examine Matty's handiwork. 'You've put windows in, I see…and that must be the door.'

'The windows is for the horses to look out,' Matty told him. 'They got to be able to see out.'

Nathan admired the barn to Matty's satisfaction and helped him herd the sheep. Then said, 'Will you play on your own for a bit, while I go and talk to your mother? I'll be back to see you in a few minutes.'

Matty nodded, content now that he was here.

Nathan stood up and drew Allie to one side, urging her towards a private corner of the L-shaped room. 'I couldn't help hearing what you said to Matty earlier,' he murmured. 'Is that the first time he's mentioned having a father around?'

'Yes, it is.' She looked at him awkwardly. 'I wasn't quite sure how to broach the subject and tell him the truth, but since he started asking questions I thought that might be a starting point. I thought I would tell him the real facts over the next week or so, as the occasion arises.' She searched his face. 'Is that all right with you?'

'I think that's a good idea. It will be better for him if he learns the truth in bits that he can take in.' He studied her thoughtfully for a moment or two, and then said, 'You didn't encourage the idea that we might live together. Does that mean you've completely discounted it?'

Her breath seemed to stick in her throat. 'I haven't discounted it. I still need to get my head around some things.'

'Such as?' He was frowning now, but before she could begin to answer they were interrupted as Owen walked into the room.

'Mum says she's finishing off the preparations for

tea and it's almost ready.' He came towards Nathan and muttered diffidently, 'You said you had some news for me when you let me in. What is it? Did you come up with something to help me when I go to court?'

Nathan gave him a quick smile. 'Yes, I did. I've had a word with Jack and he's going to apply to the court to have the case dismissed. We've had a look at some video footage from the town hall square, and it shows you sitting on a bench and talking to a friend at the time that the car was taken. There's a digital counter on the tape that shows the span of time, and you were there for well over half an hour. When you weren't on the bench you were looking at the fountain or you were standing near the shrubbery. That means you couldn't possibly be shown in the footage that the police have. You're in the clear.'

'That's wonderful news.' Allie turned to Nathan, her mouth curving in a smile, happiness shining in her eyes. Then she went to Owen and hugged him. 'I'm so relieved. Isn't it great?'

'It's brilliant.' Owen was laughing with relief, his whole manner relaxed for the first time in months. 'I can't believe it's all over. How did you do it? I told the police where I was at the time, but they didn't come up with anything to get me off the hook.'

'I went to some offices overlooking the square and had one of the managers hunt through their videotapes from the surveillance cameras. He thought the relevant one had been wiped, but an office worker found it stashed away in a cupboard. The tape had been slightly damaged, and it had been tossed to one side so that it wouldn't be used again. He was going to bin it, but then he thought his boss might want it repaired if there was anything useful on it, so he pushed it onto a shelf out of the way.'

Owen whooped with joy. 'I don't know how to thank you. It's been such a weight on my shoulders these last few weeks. I didn't know where to turn.'

Nathan sent him a lopsided grin. 'If you really want to thank me, you could think about a job interview I've lined up for you. It's for a position as a veterinary assistant in a village just a few miles from here.' His jaw moved fractionally, as though he had some vague doubts in the back of his mind. 'My parents live in the village, next door to where the vet lives, and they've become friendly with him since they moved there. My dad put in a word for you.'

'He did?' Owen blinked. 'He must have had a change of heart. How did that come about?'

'I talked to him about how you've been trying to find work, and I said you were older and wiser now.'

'Thanks. I didn't think he would ever be on my side.'

'It isn't all plain sailing. He thought it only fair to fill the vet in on your past history, but he told him how you've changed and how you're trying to get yourself together.'

Owen was doubtful. 'Won't that have put the man off? Most employers can't get past that.'

'No, he's all right with it. I went to see him, and told him the latest news, and he seemed keen to interview you. It isn't cut and dried, of course, but I really believe you're in with a good chance. You

might even get the opportunity to gain some qualifications. If he thinks you're suitable, he's willing to
send you to college for part-time study.'

'Is he?' Owen's eyes lit up. 'That's even better.
When does he want to see me?'

Nathan glanced at his watch. 'How about an hour's
time from now, at the surgery? He said he usually has
a free slot between the end of afternoon farm visits
and the evening appointments, but you'd better give
him a ring first, just to make sure that it's all right.'

He reached into his trouser pocket and drew out a
card. 'His number's on here. When I spoke to your
mother she said something about giving you a lift over
there.' He frowned as he handed over the card.
'There's a bus that runs on a regular basis between
the two villages, but we'll have to sort out some driving lessons for you, and a car, if you get the job.
Anyway, see how you go.'

'I'll go and call him now.' Owen left the room and
went to use the phone in the kitchen. Allie and Nathan
looked at each other and held their breath. Then a
minute later they heard him say to his mother. 'Are
you up to driving? Do you think you might be able to
give me a lift?'

Matty piped up hopefully, 'Where you going? Can
I come?'

Gwyneth put her head around the corner and looked
in on them. 'Is it all right if I take Matty along for the
ride? We'll stay outside, of course, while Owen goes
for his interview. I know the area, so perhaps I'll take
him for a walk along the lane.'

'Yes, that's OK.'

'Good.' Her mother frowned. 'I guess tea will have to wait.' Then she smiled and went off to get her jacket.

Allie was left alone with Nathan. 'I can't get my head around all this,' she said, shaking her head as though that would clear it. 'Everything's changed, all in the last few minutes. I'm thrilled to bits about the news.'

'He hasn't got the job yet,' Nathan warned.

'No, but he's out of trouble and he has everything to look forward to. I'm so happy. You've been so good to us, taking on Owen's problems and not pushing things about Matty. I don't deserve your kindness.'

She slid her arms around him, and hugged him, laying her cheek against his chest. His hands trailed over her back in gentle stroking movements and then he hugged her in return and she heard the tempo of his heartbeat change from a steady thud to a pounding thump-thump. After a moment or two, though, his grip on her slackened and he shifted his stance, as though he would step back from her but was reluctant to move.

She looked up at him in confusion. 'Are you all right?'

He shook his head. 'No, I don't think so. I don't think I will be ever again.'

'Why? What's wrong?' The words came out as a breathy whisper, her eyes exploring his features as though they were a gateway to his inner mind.

'I can't do this any more.' He looked down at her and there was a kind of despair written on his face.

She reached up to him, desperate to understand, her fingers tracing the line of his cheek.

'What do you mean?' She drew back from him, bewildered and out of her depth. 'Don't you want me to touch you?'

His fingers tangled in the hair at the nape of her neck. 'You have it all wrong, Allie. I want that more than anything in the world. I want you close to me. I want to be able to take you into my arms and know that everything is all right between us, that you might want me and love me in the way that I love you. But it isn't going to happen, is it? You don't feel the same way about me.'

'You love me?' The words came out as a thready sound. She scarcely dared believe what she was hearing. 'But you've never said that before…even when Matty was conceived you didn't say it. You stood back and let me go out of your life. I thought you didn't want me.'

Pain showed in his eyes. 'How could you believe that? I cared more for you than life itself, but I had to let you go. You'd just finished your first stint as senior house officer and you were heading for a new posting, miles away from where I was going to be. I couldn't hold you back. I knew how much you wanted that job. I wanted to ask you to go with me, up north, but you had everything sorted, the job was waiting for you, and you had your family to think of. I couldn't get in your way. It was the hardest thing I ever did, watching you walk away from me.'

'I had no idea you felt that way.' Her eyes clouded. 'Don't you know that I've loved you since almost the first time we met? I've always known that you were the only one for me.'

'Is that really true?' His blue eyes burned like flame, as though he dared not believe it.

'It's the truth,' she whispered. 'It broke my heart to see you go away to medical school and then go after all those specialist jobs. I didn't think we would ever be together.'

'I always came back to you. I couldn't stay away.' His fingers gripped her arms. 'I love you, Allie. I've always loved you. But every time I thought we might come together, we had to part. It was so painful, but I didn't want to hold you back. You were so young, and on the threshold of life.'

'And all the time I wanted nothing more than for you to say you loved me.' She smiled up at him, a tremulous smile edged with a growing ray of hope. 'Could we be together from now on, do you think? Is it possible?'

'But you said you weren't sure… I asked you to marry me, and it seemed as though you were turning me down.'

'I thought you only wanted to make things right for Matty. I didn't know that you loved me, and I couldn't have borne to be with you every day, sharing our lives, without that.'

'I love you.' He kissed her tenderly, and then with mounting passion, as though he couldn't get enough of her. Her head reeled with delicious sensation and she clung to him, returning the kiss in full measure. His hands stroked along the length of her, drawing her close to him, meshing her soft curves with the muscled strength of his own body. 'I need you,' he muttered, his voice thickened. He looked into her eyes. 'Will you marry me? Say that you will.'

'Yes, I will.' She gazed up at him. 'I'll marry you…I'll marry you. I love you.'

She gave herself up to his kisses, melting against him, her whole being suffused with yearning. He was everything she had ever wanted, and she longed to stay like this for ever, locked in his embrace.

They heard the sound of a car drawing up outside, and she drifted slowly back to reality.

'Your mother must be home, with Matty and Owen,' he said softly, a groan sighing in his throat. 'I hope everything went well for him. How do you think they'll react when we tell them what we've just arranged?'

'I think they'll be over the moon.' She was glowing with happiness, but one small thing marred her bliss.

'What is it?' he asked, watching the tiny frown form on her brow.

'What shall I do about my mother and Owen? She isn't terribly strong and I don't want to abandon her or Owen just as things are beginning to change for him.' She gazed at him, her expression worried.

'Well, my house is big enough for all of us. But if you think it isn't suitable, we could look for a home large enough to have a granny annexe. I suppose that way we can all be together, and yet we'll still have enough room for privacy when we want it.'

'I knew there was a reason why I love you so much,' she whispered. She reached up and kissed him once again.

Owen came and found them. He was so excited that he didn't seem to notice that they had their arms around each other, and he said in a rush, 'I got the job... I got the job...can you believe it? Can this day get any better?'

'I'm really glad for you,' Allie said, smiling happily. She glanced at Nathan, and he was grinning, too.

Her mother took a long look at the way they were standing, close together, his arm around her shoulder, her arm around his back. 'You look like a pair of conspirators,' she murmured. 'Have you two been plotting something?'

'You could say that,' Nathan answered softly. He looked into Allie's eyes and smiled.

Matty came over to them both and looked up at them, his head tilted a little to one side as though he was trying to puzzle something out. 'Are you going to be my daddy?' he asked.

'That's exactly right,' Allie said with a smile, putting her free arm around him and drawing him close. 'We're going to get married, and from now on we're all going to be together, all five of us, Nanna and Owen, too, living in one big house, and things are going to be just perfect.'

Owen and her mother exchanged exultant glances.

'A wedding,' her mother said with a laugh, 'and not before time, I might add. I was beginning to wonder if you two would ever manage to sort yourselves out.'

'Well, we did manage it...eventually.' Allie chuckled.

She looked down at Matty, her mouth curved in a smile. 'Sweetheart, Nathan's your real daddy...and we're all going to be together for always. Are you happy about that?'

Matty shot a fist in the air. 'Yes!' he shouted. 'Yes, yes, yes!'

FREE!

4 Books
and a surprise gift!

We would like to take this opportunity to thank you for reading this Mills & Boon® book by offering you the chance to take FOUR more specially selected titles from the Medical Romance™ series absolutely FREE! We're also making this offer to introduce you to the benefits of the Reader Service™—

- ★ **FREE home delivery**
- ★ **FREE gifts and competitions**
- ★ **FREE monthly Newsletter**
- ★ **Exclusive Reader Service offers**
- ★ **Books available before they're in the shops**

Accepting these FREE books and gift places you under no obligation to buy, you may cancel at any time, even after receiving your free shipment. Simply complete your details below and return the entire page to the address below. You don't even need a stamp!

YES! Please send me 4 free Medical Romance books and a surprise gift. I understand that unless you hear from me, I will receive 6 superb new titles every month for just £2.75 each, postage and packing free. I am under no obligation to purchase any books and may cancel my subscription at any time. The free books and gift will be mine to keep in any case.

M5ZEF

Ms/Mrs/Miss/Mr ....Initials...

BLOCK CAPITALS PLEASE

Surname ....

Address...

....

....Postcode ....

Send this whole page to:
UK: FREEPOST CN81, Croydon, CR9 3WZ